ACKNOWLEDGEMENTS

Writing this book was more rewarding than I could have ever imagined. I dedicate this book to my parents. My dad and pastor, the late, great, Pastor Roosevelt Campbell. To my momma, who currently resides in Florida. Without them instilling in me the love of God and to know him personally. None of this would be possible. I truly thank my Lord and Savior Jesus Christ for being my everything.

None of this would have been possible without my best friend and amazing husband, Edward. Thank you so much, babe. Your continued prayers and advice kept me focused and were instrumental in getting the book done. I love you so much.

Also, I would like to thank those three people who made me a mom. My amazing children are Eddie Jr., Angie, and Anelle. You all have kept me grounded in remembering why I do what I do. I didn't know I could love an extension of us as much as I do. Thanks for making us proud.

Thanks to my management & publicity team, Thea of T.Fielding Lowe Company, LLC, for your motivation in pushing me beyond my limits as well as your guidance. You are brilliant.

I'm eternally grateful to the strong woman in my life Lydia Campbell-Mims. Mom, I love you and admire your wisdom and strength. I thank you for being my greatest example of a woman of integrity and love of family. Delphine Cooper (Mother-In-love), thank you for all that you have done. I would also like to thank my blood sister Paula. Melody, and Rosalind. Growing up, I learned to be the best of me because your sister loves y'all to infinity and beyond.

I am thankful for my sister and brother-in-love. I have been blessed with an extended family filled with love. I'm so grateful for my godmother, aunts, uncles, cousins, nieces, nephews, church family, and friends.

Also, I would like to thank all the strong women surrounding me; Women's Groups Circles, Committees & Board members. To my Her Chronicles and Let's Pray Wednesday Intercessors, thanks for your continued support and prayers. You all are awesome!

ACKNOWLEDGEMENTS

I would like to thank all the strong women surrounding me; Women's Groups Circles, Committees & Board members. To my Her Chronicles and Let's Pray Wednesday Intercessors, thanks for your continued support and prayers. You all are awesome!

Special thanks to Pastor Sandra Miller and Dr. Phillip Miller of Shekinah Family Worship Center. For their spiritual guidance and direction as well as being my Spiritual Mentors.

Although there were periods of times in my life, filled with many ups and downs, my time writing this book of affirmations was worth it. I hit a milestone turning 50 while writing "Favored, Focused, and Fierce". I was reminded of all the promises God has made to me. I know they shall manifest. I have been commissioned to remind you to continue and strengthen your journey by reaffirming things the promises of God through his word. And remember, do the work.

A very special thanks to all of you who have supported me throughout this journey. I hope that this book brings you joy and stability within your life; empowering you to be the best version of yourself. Once again, thank you all for your continued support. Don't forget you are always "Favored, Focused, and Fierce".

FOREWORD

I am honored to share these words on behalf of this great author. I have known Angel Cooper all her life. She is a mentee and daughter of mine in addition to being an amazing wife, mother, psalmist, and motivator.

Angle Cooper is dedicated to helping people. She is a woman you want to follow on all the platforms to hear, read and experience her heartfelt healing and restoring advice.

Reading " I am Favored, Focused, and Fierce" will give you energy through her words, determination through her example of survival and victory in day-to-day real-life challenges.

God Bless you Angel on this great endeavor!
Dr. Sandra V. Miller

About Dr. Sandra V. Miller

Dr. Sandra V. Miller is a conference host and consultant. She has written "Jehovah Rapha Healing Journal" as well as created inspirational bookmarks. Dr. Miller is also the founder of Daughter of Naomi Mentoring Network in addition to being the founder and lead pastor at Shekinah Family Worship Center in Providence. RI.

AFFIRMATIONS AND DECLARATIONS
TABLE OF CONTENTS

DAY	Affirmation/Declaration
1	Everything I'm going through is developing me for my best life
2	I choose peace over pain
3	I will focus more on the good so more good will come into my life
4	I deserve to be loved and experience real love in my life
5	I am moving on because my past is over and my future is before me
6	Good things are coming for me
7	Stepping out of my comfort zone and into my purpose
8	I love me for me
9	I am enough
10	I choose peace and calmness over worry and fear
11	I deserve to be happy and healthy
12	I am happy because I know the best is yet to come for me.
13	Thank God for allowing me to make it this far
14	I am blessed; favored and loved of God
15	In every situation, I will learn and grow
16	I will speak love, hope and peace over my life
17	I am wonderfully made and created by God
18	I am worthy
19	I will celebrate every victory in my life
20	I am strong and successful because of God
21	It's ok not to be ok, because it will get better
22	I am healed and I walk in victory

AFFIRMATIONS AND DECLARATIONS
<u>TABLE OF CONTENTS</u>

<u>DAY</u>	<u>Affirmation/Declaration</u>
23	My difficult times are a part of my journey. I will learn to appreciate my Good.
24	I will show up for myself because God shows up for me
25	I will agree with the great things that are for my life
26	What I'm seeking is coming to me
27	God is giving me strength for my struggle.
28	It's ok to say no
29	I will remember that the difficult times are temporary."
30	Every day is a step toward improvement and healing
31	I'm releasing my past and pressing towards my future.
32	I am in the process of becoming the best version of myself
33	I thank God I did not give up on myself
34	I'm so glad that trouble won't last always
35	I trust and know eventually everything will be all right
36	I may have made a mistake, butI am not a mistake
37	I will be patient with myself as God is not through with me yet
38	I may not be where I want to be, but I'm not where I used to be
39	My faith is stronger than my fear
40	I am brave, bold and blessed
41	ABC's of Affirmation...I am Amazing, Brilliant & Courageous
42	I have limitless potential in Christ
43	I don't just live for things; I live to fulfill my purpose
44	I permit me to be great

AFFIRMATIONS AND DECLARATIONS
TABLE OF CONTENTS

DAY	Affirmation/Declaration
45	I'm becoming what God has for me to be every day.
46	I make a difference in the world by existing and walking in my purpose.
47	My past is not a reflection of my future
48	My Body is healthy, my mind is healthy and I'm in a healthy place
49	My life is a gift and I appreciate everything I have.
50	I am favored, focused, and forever fly

DAY 1

"Everything I'm Going Through is Developing me for My Best Life."

"I praise you because I am fearfully and wonderfully made, your works are wonderful I know that full well."

PSALM 139:14

FOUR PRACTICAL POINTS

- MAKE A VISION BOARD
- OUTLINE A PLAN OF ACTION
- FIND YOUR PURPOSE IN LIFE
- PRAYER & PERSISTENCE

Did you know that one disturbing chapter in your life does not determine your entire life story? Are you familiar with the man named Job in the Bible? He had some disturbing chapters in his life. He lost his wealth, health, and children, but he was blessed two-fold by the end of the story.

I enjoy reading a good book and anticipating what is going to happen next. When the chapters do not end exactly as I was expecting, it does not mean it is the end of the book and the story is over. It could be an indication to stay tuned that there is more to come, you may have come to a cliffhanger, or the storyline is about to change. Also, there might be a plot or character change in the next chapter. The next chapter could reveal the hero's or heroine's greatest moment. To see it unfold, we must keep reading the story and turning the pages. It is reading all the combined that make the story.

The same is true about the chapters of our lives that combine to create the entire story of life; who you are, and what you are becoming. The good, bad, and ugly. It is the culmination of it all. You are not allowed to pick and choose; deciding which chapters are good to keep. Then remove the wrong chapters. It would not make for a good read. Everything is good. Maybe that is why reality TV is so popular, because of the drama. Everyone is waiting to see a cliffhanger or a resolution. you feel like Job in the Bible. Considering all the drama you have experienced in life is developing you for your best self. When you embrace this concept, you are on your way to a more fulfilled outcome. This book of affirmations takes you on a journey reminding us to turn the page of life. When turning the page with God as your companion, it's a renewal of daily strength.

It is important to reaffirm what God says daily in order to denounce what the enemy is saying. Like our friend in the bible, Job did. *Job 13:15 (King James Version) he said, though he slays me, yet will I trust in him: but I will maintain mine own ways before him.*

It is not enough to embrace the like-able areas or chapters in life. But learn to embrace these areas accepting every chapter experience and the imprecations as Job. When I was younger, I told myself I'm too tall, too dark, and not good enough. I want to encourage you as God encouraged me. The part where you thought you were not good enough is God's same experiences in shaping you for your best self. Let us Win together, and let us Reaffirm the Promises of God over our life.

Set Your Goals

TO ACHIEVING THE PRACTICAL POINTS

GOALS

STEPS
☐
☐
☐
☐
☐
☐
☐
☐
☐

POTENTIAL PROBLEMS

STRATEGIES

PROGRESS TRACKER

Date	Progress

DAY 2

"I Choose Peace Over Pain"

"And the peace of God, which passeth all understanding, shall keep your hearts and minds through Christ Jesus."

PHILIPPIANS 4:7

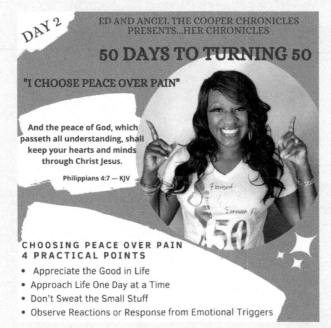

FOUR PRACTICAL POINTS

- APPRECIATE ALL THE GOOD IN LIFE
- APPROACH LIFE ONE DAY AT A TIME
- DO NOT SWEAT THE SMALL STUFF
- OBSERVE REACTIONS OR RESPONSE FROM EMOTIONAL TRIGGERS

The questions I am often asked is... how can you have peace in your life, when your life is broken into so many pieces? How are you smiling and still have peace after all you went through? Honestly, there is no magic pill. It is by the strength of God, prayer, and being around supportive people who helped. As well as applying the proper strategies (scriptures and/or affirmations) in life. This is how I have managed to survive.

As we look back at our friend Job, who had lost everything in the midst of his most challenging time. He had to reset his focus and even change his circle of friends to remind himself that God will avenge me to provide me the peace needed.

Even when all hope seems lost, God's plan for our life is to succeed. Rest in that. As I mentioned before, no one is exempt from problems and pain. Through making deliberate decisions you are securing your peace within you. Here is what that looks like. When painful life experiences interrupt or disturb your peace, such as problems or loss of marriage, illness, child (ren) loss of a parent, loved ones, and/or friend(s), loss of a business or job, etc. When pain happens, it disturbs your peace. Decide to seek the peace of God over the pain you are experiencing.

Philippians 4:6
And the peace that surpasses all understanding will guard your hearts and minds in Christ Jesus.

When Jesus decided to offer us peace, it defied the presence of pain and logic. With all the pain surrounding you, it does not seem possible that peace can be found. BUT IT CAN. On this day, you will meditate on understanding how your relationship with pain is important. Yes, I said. It is important not to hide or pretend that pain is not there. Acknowledge your pain. You cannot drink, sniff, smoke, or sleep your pain away. When you begin to practice securing your peace, it will get lodged in memory. Keep in mind, pain does not define you as a person, but your response to it does. Practice not allowing pain to consume you in thinking that suffering is all you will ever experience. You do not have to be stuck in pain forever. You can genuinely be happy from the inside out with the help of Christ. Ask Job. Follow these basic principles listed. Continue making a conscious decision to work hard at securing your peace over the pain. You will be victorious.

Set Your Goals

TO ACHIEVING THE PRACTICAL POINTS

GOALS	STEPS
	☐
	☐
POTENTIAL PROBLEMS	☐
	☐
	☐
	☐
STRATEGIES	☐
	☐
	☐
	☐

PROGRESS TRACKER

Date	Progress

DAY 3

"I will Focus More on the Good, so that More Good Things will Come into My Life."

"Give, and it shall be given unto you; good measure, pressed down, shaken together, running over, shall they give into your bosom. For with what measure ye mete it shall be measured to you again."

PHILIPPIANS 4:7

DAY 3

ED AND ANGEL THE COOPER CHRONICLES
PRESENTS...HER CHRONICLES

50 DAYS TO TURNING 50

"I WILL FOCUS MORE ON THE GOOD, SO THAT MORE GOOD THINGS WILL COME INTO MY LIFE"

"Give, and it shall be given unto you; good measure, pressed down, shaken together, running over, shall they give into your bosom. For with what measure ye mete it shall be measured to you again.
Luke 6:38 (ASV)

PRACTICAL TIPS FOR FOCUSING ON THE GOOD

1-Prayer & Meditation
2-Find a quiet place & quiet time
3-Rest & sleep is important
4- Attitude of gratitude in advance
5-Mindful of foods we eat & treatment of body

FOUR PRACTICAL POINTS

- PRAYER & MEDITATION
- FIND A QUIET PLACE & QUIET TIME
- REST & SLEEP IS IMPORTANT
- ATTITUDE OF GRATITUDE IN ADVANCE
- MINDFUL OF FOODS WE EAT & TREATMENT OF BODY

Today, I want you to become laser-focused on all of the good in your life. There are many demands that pull our focus away from the good things in life. Whether internal or external, it can be difficult to even recognize that the glass is half full and not half empty. The question then becomes, what is your perspective on your current place in life? Although pesky and painful problems in life will be unavoidable.

Do you find yourself complaining more than you do appreciating what you already have? I want you to learn to appreciate every moment in your life. Learn and grow. Do not always focus on the bad.

How can this make you better? Too often, we look at our failures and think of them as disappointments. Thinking to ourselves that, "I will never bounce back from this." I took a course in college called "Reframing Failure". I would love for you to reframe your failure by focusing on the good from mistakes made and how you could improve. Create a second chance or a reset to make things better. To quote, "start to focus on the good and more will come to you." The definition of focus is the quality of having or crisp clear visual, focal point & clear-cut. Understanding and adjusting your focus on the good things in life will allow for more good to show up which can dramatically and positively affect the things you do.

One practical way is to re-evaluate how you appreciate what you already have. Having an attitude of gratitude determines how far you go in life. It is a great way to gauge your appreciation. Being thankful for the little things creates having much in the future. For example, A steak meal is your preference, but ramen noodles are all you have in your cabinet. Appreciating having food to eat is our objective and outlook of the good. We learn to take the good with the bad. Understanding that trouble will not always last. Also, it does not warrant settling for less. It simply means being grateful for the little you have, which turns to much.

Just as the seasons change and nights turn into days; good things will show up in your life. Keep the faith. Good things will come to those who patiently hustle and wait because good is coming-through for you —-it shall be given unto you; good measure, pressed down, shaken together, running over, shall they give into your bosom. For with what measure ye mete it shall be measured to you again.

Set Your Goals

TO ACHIEVING THE PRACTICAL POINTS

GOALS	STEPS
	☐
	☐
POTENTIAL PROBLEMS	☐
	☐
	☐
	☐
STRATEGIES	☐
	☐
	☐
	☐

PROGRESS TRACKER

Date	Progress

DAY 4

"I Deserve to be Loved and Experience Real Love in My Life."

"Love is patient, and love is kind. It does not envy, it does not boast, it is not proud. It is not rude, it is not self-seeking, it is not easily angered, it keeps no record of wrongs. Love does not delight in evil but rejoices with the truth."

1 CORINTHIANS 13: 1

DAY 4

ED AND ANGEL THE COOPER CHRONICLES
PRESENTS...HER CHRONICLES

50 DAYS TO TURNING 50
"I Deserve to be Loved and Experience Real Love in my Life"

Love is patient, love is kind. It does not envy, it does not boast, it is not proud. It is not rude, it is not self-seeking, it is not easily angered, it keeps no record of wrongs. Love does not delight in evil but rejoices with the truth.

1 Corinthians 13: 1

Here's why....
I deserve love and to experience real love in my life.

• Love is Non- Controlling or Manipulative
• Love is Understanding & Forgiving
• Love Is Honest & Respects boundaries
• Love is Willing and Open to try Together

FOUR PRACTICAL POINTS

- LOVE IS NON-CONTROLLING OR MANIPULATIVE
- LOVE IS UNDERSTANDING & FORGIVING
- LOVE IS HONEST & RESPECTS BOUNDARIES
- LOVE IS WILLING AND OPEN TO TRYING TOGETHER

Relationships are complex and can be more complicated when you are with the wrong folks. Trying to understand the depth of God's love for us is heaven sent; literally. Christ gave his life at a cost that no one could ever repay. I am not even sure if you are aware that you deserve to be loved. You deserve to experience real love in your life; from others, including yourself.

Love is an action word that requires effort. I have been married to Ed, my high school sweetheart, for 29 years. When we wrote our book, "Love is Worth the Work"; our foundation scripture used was love is patient and love is kind. It can sometimes be challenging to be open to receiving or giving love after being hurt, especially with so many storybook fantasies of love. My prayer for you is that you would never give up or turn your back on true love cause real love exists. True love gives of oneself. Today, I need you to reaffirm and meditate on these words. I deserve to be loved and experience real love in my life. I deserve to be loved and I will love myself. I deserve real love in life and the great things that come with it. When you have encountered the wrong kinds of love, it sometimes shields you from being open in believing real love exists for you. You have a choice to either settle, make excuses or decide what you will accept for your life, in your life, and your relationships; CHOOSE WISELY.

I was coaching a young woman, who was on the dating scene. I suggested she consider this theory. When you see something you dislike while dating someone, consider it a red flag. In relationships, the red flag represents an action or statement that makes you uncomfortable. You need to pause. Do not be a collector of red flags. A red light is an indicator to stop and evaluate what is going on around you. Honor the red flags as it indicates that you need to address this action or statement. Handle them calmly.

If there is real change taking place, follow the transformation of your relationship. You are not a collector of red flags. Today we affirm... We will no longer make excuses for people who canceled out on us in love.
I encourage you to honor the signs, recognize what you see, and realize that you deserve real love in your life of that love coming from you first.

Set Your Goals

TO ACHIEVING THE PRACTICAL POINTS

GOALS

STEPS
☐
☐
☐
☐
☐
☐
☐
☐
☐

POTENTIAL PROBLEMS

STRATEGIES

PROGRESS TRACKER

Date	Progress

DAY 5

<u>"I Am Moving On Because my Past is Over, and my future is before me."</u>

"I press on toward the goal to win the prize for which God has called me heavenward in Christ Jesus."

PHILIPPIANS 3:14

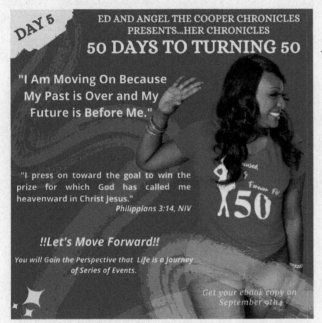

FOUR PRACTICAL POINTS

- MOVING FORWARD IS NECESSITY
- PERMIT YOURSELF TO FEEL WHAT YOU FEEL
- IF YOU ARE FEELING STUCK; SPEAK WITH SOMEONE
- GET A PERSPECTIVE; LIFE IS A JOURNEY OF SERIES OF EVENTS

When you decide to move on in life, it means you have made a conscious decision to understand your current state. You see, your future is brighter than your past. In Genesis 19:6, there is a story of Lot's wife, who was unwilling to move forward. What happens when she turns back? Let's say it turned out to be a salty ending.

A big part of not moving on is the unwillingness and the acceptance of forgiveness. Forgiveness of those who miss treated you and forgiveness for yourself. Acceptance-meaning that it was not my fault what happened. It happened. Recognize that if you remain stuck in fear, trauma, or unforgiveness, you won't receive healing or the blessings that are in store for you. This concept of accepting is to feel, shame, or hatred. It is all right when placed in its proper context. The Bible even says in the book of Ephesians 4:26 Be ye angry, and sin not: let not the sun go down upon your wrath.

Continuing to carry the heavyweight of your pain, will show up in your life in different ways. Physically, mentally, spiritually, and emotionally as a hindrance to being healed from your pain of the past. Remember to release and let it go to God. When pain and shame begin to manifest themselves in your life, that is a sure sign it may be time for you to release some of those toxic emotional connections and move forward to a healing place.

When dealing with trauma in my life, I recognized that I put on about 15 extra pounds. I was not my best self and I needed to do something about being stuck in this place. I felt like I was stuck in a dark room and I could not locate the light switch. When Christ sent me a lifeline, either from a song, reading the word, my mentor, or my spiritual leader. It was as if the light switch had turned on and the room became bright again. I was able to see clearer and I received strength from God to take each day step-by-step. I'm glad I did not spiral completely out of control as I was in my dark place. God showed up right on time and removed the things from my life so that I could get laser focus again on what truly mattered. Maybe it did not work out at that job, that marriage, that business plan, that relationship, but I encourage you to keep moving forward because your past is over and your future is before you. Do not be like Lot's wife in the Bible; stuck and unable to move forward.

Set Your Goals

TO ACHIEVING THE PRACTICAL POINTS

GOALS	STEPS

GOALS

STEPS

- [ ]
- [ ]
- [ ]
- [ ]
- [ ]
- [ ]
- [ ]
- [ ]
- [ ]
- [ ]

POTENTIAL PROBLEMS

STRATEGIES

PROGRESS TRACKER

Date	Progress

DAY 6

"Good Things are Coming for Me."

"And whatever you ask in prayer, you will receive if you have faith."

MATTHEW 21:22

FOUR PRACTICAL POINTS

- REMAIN POSITIVE
- REMAIN FOCUSED AND KEEP GOING
- REMEMBER TO TREAT OTHERS WELL
- REALIZE YOU DESERVE GOOD IN YOUR LIFE

How you choose to believe and speak life will determine what comes back to you. The words we speak manifest in our lives. Words have power, words have influence, and words are molecules that affect the atmosphere. What you desire and focus on has a way of coming back to you, positive or negative. In today's affirmation and declaration, we declare and decree that good things are coming for me and you. I am certain Abraham and Sarah in the Bible thought at their age; having a baby was never going to happen. Yet good things arrived. Read about it in Genesis 21.

There is a saying, "what you believe is what you attract". The Bible says —whatever you ask and pray; you will receive if you have faith. I want to share with you what faith is. It is the complete trust or confidence in someone or something. Faith believes in a particular thing without sure proof. I may not see it, but I believe that I will receive it. "With my mouth, I reaffirm that one day my business will be listed in Forbes magazine. I will have multiple companies and streams of income. My marriage will continually be blessed as well as myself and my husband. I believe that all of my family will be saved. I will be healthy, happy and a multi-billionaire. My children, my children's children, and their lineage will not want for anything." These words are an example of speaking, working towards my goals in faith, and believing all your good requests are coming to you.

When I ask God in prayer, God promises to give me the desires of my heart. The same applies to you. If you have faith the size of a mustard seed, your faith can move mountains. Your confidence can manifest good things in your life. Trials will come to distract you, but the word is true. You can have whatever you ask in prayer. God's words have power. They are the promises he made to us, the believers, of his word. "We declare over and over again that good things are coming for me. Good things are coming for me. Good things are coming for me. Good things are coming for me!"

Allow me to remind you that the enemy's job is to kill, steal, and destroy your vision and life. He will do everything to distract you from believing your life will always be wrong. I pray that the enemy's hand is canceled out of your life and that good shall find you. Remember to counteract those negative thoughts with the scriptures. Your God is greater than any circumstance. Your God is greater than any problem and the good is coming for you. Abraham and Sarah will attest to God's faithfulness.

Set Your Goals

TO ACHIEVING THE PRACTICAL POINTS

GOALS	STEPS
	☐
	☐
POTENTIAL PROBLEMS	☐
	☐
	☐
STRATEGIES	☐
	☐
	☐
	☐

PROGRESS TRACKER

Date	Progress

DAY 7

<u>"I'm Stepping Out of My Comfort Zone and Into My Purpose."</u>

"Have I not commanded you? Be strong and courageous. Do not be frightened, and do not be dismayed, for the Lord your God is with you wherever you go."

JOSHUA 1:9

FOUR PRACTICAL POINTS

- FACE YOUR FEAR
- MAKE A LIST OF THE THINGS YOU WANT TO OVERCOME
- STEPPING OUT WILL BENEFIT YOU
- DON'T ALLOW THE PRESSURE TO OVERWHELM YOU

When God told Ed and me to move from our home in Rhode Island to Georgia after living there for all of our lives, we were taking a huge risk. Honestly, I was scared. All I ever knew was Rhode Island. We both had retired and gotten comfortable. But God had other plans. I did not think I could step out of my comfort zone not knowing what to expect. We began to pray and seek direction and instructions. At one point, we questioned God because it was at the height of the pandemic.

"Are you sure this is what you want, God?" The reality is, stepping outside of your everyday routine or comfort zone is scary, but if God is for you, no one can be against you. Making excuses or running away will not change the heart or mind of God. It is best to follow his lead and that is what did. In the

Bible, when God appointed Joshua to succeed Moses. Joshua was successful because he was a faithful follower. Read Joshua 1.

Even though Ed and I delayed obedience, we decided to take baby steps towards this direction for our lives as well as our family's lives. We started to share with others what God told us to do in prayer and we began connecting to establish plans for the move. I can honestly say it has stretched us entirely out of our comfort zone into the area of blessings and overflow; due to our obedience. When we stopped worrying about how everything will unfold and decided to trust God, our fear was no longer an issue.

We developed a mindset that if God said to do it that settles it. We have to do it. Our mustard seed faith became big as a tree. We started to walk more courageously in the areas we did not walk tall in before. We saw the effects of open doors and the overflow of blessings. I encourage you today too. Apply the strategies for this affirmation to assist you in stepping out of your comfort zone with Christ and into your overflow of blessings because of obedience.

Set Your Goals

TO ACHIEVING THE PRACTICAL POINTS

GOALS	STEPS
	☐
	☐
	☐
POTENTIAL PROBLEMS	☐
	☐
	☐
	☐
STRATEGIES	☐
	☐
	☐

PROGRESS TRACKER

Date	Progress

DAY 8

<u>"I Love Me for Me."</u>

"Whoever gets sense loves his soul; he who keeps understanding will discover good."

PROVERBS 19:8

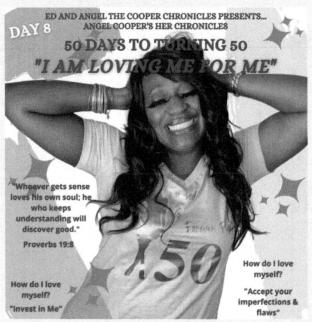

FOUR PRACTICAL POINTS

- INVEST IN THE ACTIONS TO LOVE YOU
- BE PRESENT FOR YOURSELF
- ACCEPT YOUR IMPERFECTIONS & FLAWS
- CELEBRATE ALL YOUR VICTORIES; GREAT & SMALL

Why are we worried about measuring up to someone else's expectations instead of loving ourselves for who we are and what we have to offer? I was thinking about how Moses felt so inadequate for the work he did in Exodus 4:10. Still, God chose him for the assignment.

We do not need anyone else to put us down because we do a great job doing that ourselves. I know I did. Ultimately, we are the one who determines our state of mind. Choose to make a conscious decision, saying "I will love me". Today, invest in the effort of your well-being to love you for yourself.

In this affirmation and declaration, I will encourage you to begin to love yourself completely. Loving is the beginning of improving your relationships. In Proverbs 19:8, the Bible verse we used for this day explores the concept that loving one's soul will do you good. Loving yourself connects you with the ability to love others. You show up for your true self, being nice and forgiving yourself. Once we get the concept, we will see self-appreciation extends to others, but it must first begin with oneself.

Figuring out what self-love looks like, let's explore what it is not. It is not conditional or not based on how you look— it's CONSISTENT. I practice and accept myself. You will notice imperfections, but it's what makes you your authentic self.

We encourage you to love yourself as Christ has loved us without conditions. If you are looking for the answers on how to love yourself, open your heart to God. He will send you answers. You are worth fighting for overtime. Connecting with yourself is the best thing that could have ever happened. I encourage you to be kind to yourself as much as others request that from you.

Take inventory as you cultivate the same love expected of others in your life. In doing so, it is all right to let go of the toxic things and people in your life. When you invest in loving yourself, you do not intentionally harm yourself. You care for yourself, so keep that in mind. Today I challenge you to continue loving you from a pure place. Bring your family and the world the best qualities deserving the best you have, most importantly loving you for you.

Set Your Goals

TO ACHIEVING THE PRACTICAL POINTS

GOALS	STEPS
	☐
	☐
POTENTIAL PROBLEMS	☐
	☐
	☐
	☐
STRATEGIES	☐
	☐
	☐
	☐

PROGRESS TRACKER

Date	Progress

"I Am Enough."

"And He has said to me, 'My grace is sufficient for you, for power is perfected in weakness.' Most gladly, therefore, I will rather boast about my weaknesses, so that the power of Christ may dwell in me. Therefore I am well content with weaknesses, with insults, with distresses, with persecutions, with difficulties, for Christ's sake; for when I am weak, then I am strong."

2 CORINTHIANS 12:9-10

FOUR PRACTICAL POINTS

- ACCEPTANCE OF YOURSELF
- EMBRACE WHAT IT MEANS TO BE ENOUGH
- REFRAME YOUR FAILURES AS LESSONS LEARNED
- STOP THE NEGATIVE & PROMOTE POSITIVE THINKING

Who gets to decide that you are not enough anyway? Why listen to them, unless it is God? He is the only one whose word counts. Let me reassure you-you are MORE THAN ENOUGH. Your steps are ordered. God will qualify you for whatever it is that he has called you to do. I could not help but think of Rahab in the Bible. You can read about it in Joshua: 1:1-21. A harlot turned hero in the Bible. We still talk about her being enough today.

We long and crave acceptance from others. From this day forward, I encourage you to accept yourself. I remember in elementary school at gym time, waiting to be picked or chosen

I for the team. As I waited for my chance, I thought that I was not good enough for the team. I made up my mind that I did not meet the standard because I was chosen last. Even as adults, we go back to those feelings and experiences. Not sufficient for the relationship, job, or assignment. Yes, you are different, but that is what makes you; you.

The reasons people hesitate are because you shine with purpose; so shine anyway. In embracing your difference(s), do not diminish your shine or glow. You are enough to do whatever it is that you put your mind to. Continue to be humble and gracefully respond to those who want to make you feel less than.

I encourage self-development; building on the mindset that you are enough. Study the areas that you want to grow in and walk boldly into the blessings of God. The grace of God will take you where the favor of God won't keep you. Remember you are more than enough for your assignment with Christ. Learn to Trust God as Rahab did.

Set Your Goals

TO ACHIEVING THE PRACTICAL POINTS

GOALS	STEPS
	☐
	☐
POTENTIAL PROBLEMS	☐
	☐
	☐
	☐
STRATEGIES	☐
	☐
	☐
	☐

PROGRESS TRACKER

Date	Progress

DAY 10

"I Choose Peace and Calmness Over Worry and Fear."

"Peace I leave with you; my peace I give to you. Not as the world gives do I give to you. Let not your hearts be troubled, neither let them be afraid."

JOHN 14:27

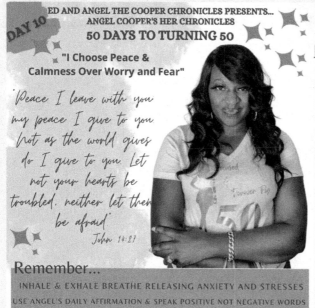

ED AND ANGEL THE COOPER CHRONICLES PRESENTS...
ANGEL COOPER'S HER CHRONICLES
50 DAYS TO TURNING 50
DAY 10
"I Choose Peace & Calmness Over Worry and Fear"

"Peace I leave with you my peace I give to you not as the world gives do I give to you. Let not your hearts be troubled, neither let then be afraid" John 14:27

Remember...
INHALE & EXHALE BREATHE RELEASING ANXIETY AND STRESSES
USE ANGEL'S DAILY AFFIRMATION & SPEAK POSITIVE NOT NEGATIVE WORDS

FOUR PRACTICAL POINTS

- INHALE & EXHALE; BREATHE RELEASING ANXIETY AND STRESS
- TAKE A WALK
- USE ANGEL'S DAILY AFFIRMATION & SPEAK POSITIVELY
- REST, RESTORE, RESET

Life is about choices. The choices we make will impact our future. Why is it when you choose what is best for you, like seeking peace and ignoring the drama, people get upset with you? Why? It is not their decision. It is your choice. I do not understand why they get upset.

I want you to have the courage to do the right thing. This may not always be the easiest but the best move. In the moment of decision making, consider your options determining long or short-term impact. In today's affirmation with all the pressure in the surrounding world and personal circumstances, having peace is a necessity for life. I was thinking about David how in Samuel 17, he chooses the peace of God to defeat Goliath. When you are unsure and need to make a decision, asking God for help in small or big ways is a smart move. For instance, how I respond to my husband or children when I am upset. The impact of words once it leaves your mouth can be devastating. You cannot take back words. Practice asking God in prayer, how to guard my peace during intense moments. We can always apologize, but whether big or small choices, ask God for help in your decision-making process. You can never go wrong.

Many times are choosing to do the right things. You are an inspiration in choosing the wrong. You are penalized. Then endless guilts of thoughts and why invade our conscious. Consider this. Even those who are fearful in the most pressing choices consult God then decide on what to do.
No one is perfect. It is important to do the proper thing. Your spouse, children, family, or business can be affected by the wrong decision you make. Please, take a deep breath. Choose peace over drama, be calm and rely on Christ instead of worry and fear. Exercise peace and calmness daily.

Here are a few strategies with practical ways in approaching this process. Continue to educate yourself on seeking the guidance of others. Remember to eliminate the fear. Activate your trust in God in order to kill Giants as David did.

TODAY'S AFFIRMATION & DECLARATION

Set Your Goals

TO ACHIEVING THE PRACTICAL POINTS

GOALS	STEPS

POTENTIAL PROBLEMS

STRATEGIES

- [ ]
- [ ]
- [ ]
- [ ]
- [ ]
- [ ]
- [ ]
- [ ]
- [ ]

PROGRESS TRACKER

Date	Progress

DAY 11

"I Deserve to be Happy and Healthy."

"Delight thyself also in the LORD; and he shall give thee the desires of thine heart."

PSALMS 37:4

As I turn 50, I have made a conscious decision to choose myself. No, I am not being arrogant. I recognize I cannot pour from an empty pitcher. Making a stand in choosing to be happy and healthy does not just benefit me, but helps others around me.

Naomi, in the Bible, wanted to be happy after losing her husband and son. God granted her heart's desire. (Read Ruth 4:14-15) Gone are the days I believed choosing me was selfish. I now know that not choosing me was inadequate self-care. I only wished someone shared this with me sooner while raising my children or in the early stages of my marriage. I am now a big advocate of self-care. I have an initiative called "Self Care Saturdays". On Saturdays, I share a list of self-care activities that support women mentally, spiritually, and emotionally.

There are times when medical self-care is not the only thing needed to reset your thinking. God has been my source, teaching me gracefully how to hold onto my peace and weeding out negative thoughts. Being a certified coach, I have learned through study, fostering positive emotions can change our outlook and outcome. We can take steps to jumpstart our happiness and change the culture of our surroundings in a practical approach.

Sometimes, it is within that negative cycle that we need healing. The cycle can be a direct result of our thinking. Inactivity, lack of exercise, or fitness can contribute to a lull or unhappiness. Certain foods can also make us feel sluggish when we're in search of our happy place. It may taste great going down. Then we crash, coming off our sugar happy high. Considering small changed behaviors can have a direct positive result.

God is my greatest source of joy. He is consistent. Nor food or drink; can satisfy me like my relationship with him. Love you enough to know that God created you. He knows what you need. I challenge you to come to know him, ask him in your life, and observe the turnaround- Sinners prayer. Romans 10:9-10 says that "if you declare with your mouth, "Jesus is Lord," and believe in your heart that God raised him from the dead, you will be saved. For it is with your heart that you believe and is justified, and it is with your mouth that you profess your faith and are saved.
I share with you in hopes you will receive a Happy Healthy Life in Christ, not free of issues, just strength to endure.

Set Your Goals

TO ACHIEVING THE PRACTICAL POINTS

GOALS	STEPS
	☐

POTENTIAL PROBLEMS

STRATEGIES

PROGRESS TRACKER

Date	Progress

DAY 12

"I Am Happy, because I Know The Best is Yet to Come for Me."

"But as it is written, Eye hath not seen, nor ear heard, neither have entered into the heart of man, the things which God hath prepared for them that love him."

1 CORINTHIANS 2:9

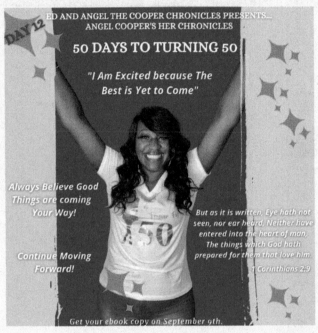

FOUR PRACTICAL POINTS

- REMAIN FOCUSED ON THE GOOD
- THE WILLINGNESS TO CHANGE
- HAPPY FOR OTHERS SUCCESS
- BE A LIFELONG LEARNER

One of my favorite phrases is "The Best is Yet To Come". It is an expression that means; yes, you have good and bad experiences happen in your life, but whatever is happening in the present and future will surpass the past. I choose to believe that God has something better for my family. Again, this reminds me of our friend Job in the Bible. After his struggle in Job 42, God restored him. Remember the best is yet to come!

Even in the darkest hour or in my most challenging situation, I wanted to believe that God had the best in mind for me. In today's affirmations, I want you to activate your faith. Faith is the primary ingredient to a relationship with God. The Bible says in Hebrew 11 faith is the substance of things hoped for and the evidence of things not seen. Understanding faith allows you to recognize this affirmation. It is impossible to please God and understand his precepts, steps, or life plans without faith.

My faith helps me to understand that your present situation will not be your final destination. There is more joy, more peace, and more hope. Today's scripture says eyes have not seen, neither have the ears heard all the things God has in store to them that love God. If you do, he's promised you his best. He will show you incredible things in life. The question is, are you open and willing to receive the Greater?

When pressing towards your goals in life, you are heading in an upward motion. Keep in mind that continue looking up, continue moving up, and ascending up in life to reach the best God has in store for you.

Set Your Goals

TO ACHIEVING THE PRACTICAL POINTS

GOALS	STEPS
	☐
	☐
	☐
POTENTIAL PROBLEMS	☐
	☐
	☐
	☐
STRATEGIES	☐
	☐
	☐

PROGRESS TRACKER

Date	Progress

DAY 13

"Thank God for Allowing me to Make it This Far."

"But grow in the grace and knowledge of our Lord and Savior Jesus Christ. To him be the glory both now and to the day of eternity. Amen."

2 PETER 3:18

FOUR PRACTICAL POINTS

- APPRECIATE YOURSELF & YOUR UNIQUENESS
- GIVE YOURSELF SOME GRACE
- YOU HAVE MADE PROGRESS IN THE PROCESS
- REFRAME YOUR FAILURES AS LESSONS LEARNED

I remember being in Georgia after living in Rhode Island all my life. I looked around with tears of joy because I knew nobody, but God who blessed us with the homes, jobs (now though retired), health, and some wealth. Was I expecting more great things to happen in life? Absolutely, but I decided to be thankful for what I had and not to complain. There was a song my aunt would sing. "I've had some good days. I've had some hills to climb. I've had some weary days and sleepless nights. When I look around and think things over, all of my good days outweigh my bad days. I choose not to complain." It is at that moment, I lift my eyes to heaven and say, thank you, Lord. I am about to turn 50 years young. I understand that some of my family members and friends did not get this far.

I truly thank God for everything because it was developing me for my greater good. There were times for me and I am sure it's for you too. Wanting to give up, walk away and throw away the towel. I believed God would throw it back and say wipe your tears and keep it moving.

There is always a process of making mistakes along the way. Forgive yourself, pray to God and move on. Thank him for everything and celebrate every milestone. Remember, you made it to this point. Appreciate your achievements and accomplishments and stay forever thankful. Having an attitude of gratitude, God will bless you with more.

Set Your Goals

TO ACHIEVING THE PRACTICAL POINTS

GOALS	STEPS
	☐
	☐
	☐

POTENTIAL PROBLEMS

☐
☐
☐
☐
☐

STRATEGIES

☐
☐

PROGRESS TRACKER

Date	Progress

DAY 14

<u>"I Am Blessed; Favored and Loved of God."</u>

"And the angel came in unto her, and said, Hail, thou that art highly favored, the Lord is with thee: blessed art thou among women."

LUKE 1:28

ED AND ANGEL THE COOPER CHRONICLES PRESENTS...
ANGEL COOPER'S HER CHRONICLES
DAY 14
50 DAYS TO TURNING 50

"I Am Blessed; Favored and Loved of God"

"Know God deeply Loves you"

"Learn to Trust God When you Can't Trace Him"

And the angel came in unto her, and said, Hail, thou that art highly favored, the Lord is with thee: blessed art thou among women.
Luke 1:28

Get your ebook copy on September 9th.

FOUR PRACTICAL POINTS

- KNOW GOD LOVES YOU DEEPLY
- LEARN TO TRUST GOD WHEN YOU CAN'T FIND HIM
- ALWAYS BELIEVE THE LORD WANTS THE BEST FOR YOU
- HAVE THE HEART TO SERVE THE LORD

There have been many times when we have looked into the mirror and did not like what we saw looking back at us. Maybe we were having a bad hair day, or our outfit does not fit our bodies right. Regardless of our outward appearance, just know that how the Lord feels about us will never change.

The important thing in this moment is to reflect on how God sees you. Today's affirmation is a gentle reminder to use your spiritual lens to focus. In the Bible, Job 13, Job said "I would trust God". He was distressed by leprosy and loss. He understood that he was loved by God. Take note and trust God through it.

God sees you as the "blessed of God", "favored of God", and

"loved of God". Allow God's visual of us to marinate within our soul. We can approach life differently. The blessings of God are likened to a door. Being thankful or grateful for the small blessings will open doors to many more Blessings.

When God shines his favor in your life, it is a display of his mercy and goodness. It is visual and tangible evidence of God's care and love in your life. No matter who you are or what you have done, God has his best intentions for you to commit to his plan and will for your life.

Set Your Goals

TO ACHIEVING THE PRACTICAL POINTS

GOALS	STEPS
	☐
	☐
POTENTIAL PROBLEMS	☐
	☐
	☐
	☐
STRATEGIES	☐
	☐
	☐
	☐

PROGRESS TRACKER

Date	Progress

DAY 15

"In Every Situation, I will Learn and Grow."

"Show me your ways, LORD, teach me your paths."

PSALM 25:4

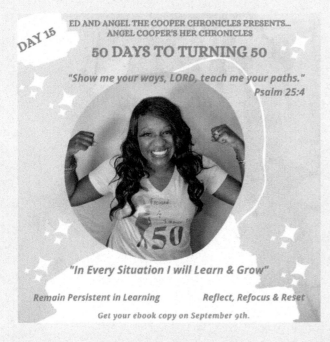

ED AND ANGEL THE COOPER CHRONICLES PRESENTS...
ANGEL COOPER'S HER CHRONICLES

50 DAYS TO TURNING 50

DAY 15

"Show me your ways, LORD, teach me your paths."
Psalm 25:4

"In Every Situation I will Learn & Grow"

Remain Persistent in Learning   Reflect, Refocus & Reset

Get your ebook copy on September 9th.

FOUR PRACTICAL POINTS

- REMAIN PERSISTENT IN LEARNING
- REFLECT, REFOCUS & RESET
- KEEP A POSITIVE PERSPECTIVE
- EXPECT CHALLENGES & SETBACKS

Today's affirmation will demonstrate how to ask God about everything. "Show me your ways and teach me your path." Having the strength of God in every situation does not eliminate problems but gives a better response to them. Using his wisdom approach, if you have a setback, do not take a step back but get ready for your comeback.

Learning how to reframe your mistakes and failures into lessons learned is the purpose of today. For example, the last chapter of life did not go as planned. It is not time to stop. The approach is to turn the page and keep moving forward because trouble won't always last, and it will get better.

Although our problems are very present and real. Problems are not permanent. Ask God for strength, wisdom, and assistance. I guarantee he will and provide. Be willing not only to just learn from everything you experience but to grow from it as well.

Set Your Goals

TO ACHIEVING THE PRACTICAL POINTS

GOALS	STEPS

☐

☐

☐

☐

☐

☐

☐

☐

☐

POTENTIAL PROBLEMS

STRATEGIES

PROGRESS TRACKER

Date	Progress

DAY 16

"I will Speak Love, Hope and Peace Over My Life."

"Death and life are in the power of the tongue: and they that love it shall eat the fruit thereof."

PROVERBS 18:21

ED AND ANGEL THE COOPER CHRONICLES PRESENTS...
ANGEL COOPER'S HER CHRONICLES

50 DAYS TO TURNING 50

"I Will Speak Love, Hope & Peace over my Life"

Death and life are in the power of the tongue: and they that love it shall eat the fruit thereof.

Proverbs 18:21

"Know Words have Power"

"Build up Don't Tear Down"

Get your ebook copy on September 9th.

FOUR PRACTICAL POINTS

- KNOW WORDS HAVE POWER
- BUILD UP; DON'T TEAR DOWN
- REMAIN INTENTIONAL OF POSITIVE SPEECH
- SPEAK GOD'S WORD IN YOUR LIFE

One of the best tools of God's word is the application of his promises. I am praying, speaking, reading, declaring, and reaffirming his words over our lives. In doing this, it is crucial to align his promises with exactly what we are going through in our lives; even though the promise is the opposite of what is happening to you. Results will turn in your favor. It begins with the mindset that if God says it, then that settles it. Affirm that you will speak love, hope, and peace throughout my life.

When I was younger, I remember my father and mother said I could do anything I set my mind to do. As I turn 50, those exact words still resonate in my life today, as negative comments others who aren't as positive are spoken to meWords hurt or can give strength. A single word can create or destroy its power whether negative orpositive. In Proverbs 18:21, God says that we have death or life in the power of the tongue. Words shape and create our reality.

The Bible also says, "Let there be light". God spoke it into existence. The sound became form. Words have power, so be careful to watch how you talk about your situations, spouses, children, or yourself. Consider how you want to define the world you live in? Speak the promises over your life. Being consistent in this practice will begin to transform you daily.

Today, you will discover the power of God's work in your life by the words that you speak.
Do not miss this point, God will speak to you through his word. As you read the Bible, you can boldly hear him speak to you. Spend time in prayer and listening in reading his word.
His instructions will become evident. It will be our choice to listen, speak and live his word as well as manifest the promises for our lives.

Set Your Goals

TO ACHIEVING THE PRACTICAL POINTS

GOALS	STEPS
	☐
	☐

POTENTIAL PROBLEMS

☐
☐
☐

STRATEGIES

☐
☐
☐
☐

PROGRESS TRACKER

Date	Progress

DAY 17

"I am Wonderfully Made and Created by God."

"I will praise thee; for I am fearfully and wonderfully made: marvelous are thy works; and that my soul knoweth right well."

PSALM 139:14

FOUR PRACTICAL POINTS

- GOD IS ALWAYS PURPOSEFUL ON CREATION
- HONOR THE CREATOR WITH SERVICE TO HIM
- REGARDLESS OF HOW WE FEEL YOU ARE NO MISTAKE
- YOU ARE A PRICELESS MASTERPIECE

The scripture states that we are fearfully made. It does not mean that we are scared of being afraid. Actually, it is the very opposite. With great reverence and heartfelt interest, we were uniquely designed. Every person was created in the mind of Christ with a unique purpose. Since a man has a choice of free will is the reason for sin in the world. The word says wonderfully made. Know that we are set aside or set apart for his use.

Christ has a design for our lives, regardless of our present or past history. In honoring his purpose for your life, he will honor and bless you. In today's affirmation, recognize his design then be obedient to his will and plan. It is never too late to walk in the fullness of God's love for you. Every day is an opportunity to get closer to our creator and father. Throughout the obedience of Job in the Bible, God gave him an expected blessed end in life. You got this because God got you.

Our negative thoughts like to make us feel unworthy or not good enough for God's love. The enemy's job is to kill, steal and destroy, so he sets out to make us feel hopeless. His intention is to make us begin to doubt God's plan of being wonderful and worthy of the best life he has to offer. If the enemy can get our focus off the Lord then he has defeated us.

Today, we have been made aware of his tricks and schemes. We will never fall for that manipulation. God says who we are; we just have to believe it. Every time you feel the disappointment rising up within, making you believe the rejections and pain, combat it with the word of God. Declare his power! Declare his mercy! Declare God's best for you! God is faithful to his word, so trust him through any negative moments. He will restore your promises of life by using these affirmations.

Set Your Goals

TO ACHIEVING THE PRACTICAL POINTS

GOALS	STEPS
	☐
	☐
POTENTIAL PROBLEMS	☐
	☐
	☐
	☐
STRATEGIES	☐
	☐
	☐
	☐

PROGRESS TRACKER

Date	Progress

DAY 18

"I Am Worthy."

"For we are God's masterpiece. He has created us anew in Christ Jesus, so we can do the good things he planned for us long ago."

EPHESIANS 2:10

FOUR PRACTICAL POINTS

- NEVER SETTLE FOR WHAT YOU DON'T DESERVE
- SPEND TIME WITH THOSE WHO VALUE YOU
- HAVING SELF-RESPECT FOR YOURSELF & AWARENESS YOU DESERVE RESPECT
- DO NOT BE SO HARD ON YOURSELF

I want you to know that you are worthy of all the good God has for you. Now, I want you to believe you are worthy of this, regardless of how imperfect we feel or how our insecurities scream out. It will never change the fact that you are worthy and deserving of love and every good thing. Take courage and say, "I am worthy." You are worthy even if some things are left unfinished during the day. You are still worthy of good in your life. In Job's suffering, he forced himself to look past the present pain to his promises and worth in God.

The question is, "what is our worth"? It requires us to know our worthiness. The definition of worth is the value equivalent to that of someone or something under consideration. The level at which someone or something is under consideration. The level at which someone or somethingdeserves to bevalued or rated.

In today's affirmation, declare "I AM WORTHY!" Ephesians 2:10, (New Living Translation) says for we are God's masterpiece, he has created us anew in Christ Jesus, so we can do the good things he planned for us long ago.

Keep in mind, the plan that God has made for you. You are a masterpiece. You are valued more than you give yourself credit. When you feel less of a person, I need you to repeat these affirmations and watch the videos again. Recite the affirmations with confidence. "I am worthy of love in my life. I am worthy of God's good. I am worthy of blessings in my life. I AM WORTHY".

Every day think about your worthiness. Claim your value and never forget how God sees you. From mess to a masterpiece, from your test to testimony, from forgotten to forgive. You deserve the best of God. You are worthy. We are focused, we are favored & we-are- forever fly.

Set Your Goals

TO ACHIEVING THE PRACTICAL POINTS

GOALS	STEPS
	☐

POTENTIAL PROBLEMS

☐

☐

☐

STRATEGIES

☐

☐

☐

☐

☐

PROGRESS TRACKER

Date	Progress

DAY 19

"I will Celebrate Every Victory in My Life."

"But thanks be to God, which giveth us victory through our Lord Jesus Christ."

1 CORINTHIANS 15:57

FOUR PRACTICAL POINTS

- ENJOY THE JOURNEY TO YOUR DESTINATION
- THANK GOD FOR THE COURAGE & CONFIDENCE
- ACCOUNTABILITY TO GOALS, ENERGY & MOTIVATION
- NEVER STOP LEARNING & MAKING IMPROVEMENTS

I have three children. I can recall when they all began to walk. I remember picking up the phone to call my family to share this milestone with them. Even if it was one step or three; we cheered, screamed, and were so proud of them. Learning how to celebrate your small or significant milestones is essential to your progress. In today's affirmation, I will celebrate every victory in my life. I will show you why it is important to celebrate.

Having an appreciation for the determination and inspiration to move forward even when it gets tough is worthy of celebration. Whether it is in school, business, life, or any challenge. Celebrating small victories and accomplishments should be recognized. Today's affirmation permits you to say to yourself or to those you; good job. Those words to you or someone you care about encourages them to go further.

Taking a pause, to say, I see all the hard work and effort you are giving. Allows a time of reset or refreshing of strength in order to receive your second wind to continue. Hard work is hard work. My husband shared that when I told him he was doing a great job at cooking. He is convinced a professional chef has nothing on his meals. My words to him were a boost to his confidence as well as acknowledge the work he was doing for his family.

We have been so used to downplaying our wins. Using a perfect combination of humbleness and gratefulness. I encourage you to take time to celebrate your achievements in life and with others around you. Even if they are small victories, celebrate them anyway. God has given you the strength to succeed, so thank him for the blessings.

Set Your Goals

TO ACHIEVING THE PRACTICAL POINTS

GOALS	STEPS
	☐

POTENTIAL PROBLEMS

STRATEGIES

☐ ☐ ☐ ☐ ☐ ☐ ☐ ☐ ☐

PROGRESS TRACKER

Date	Progress

DAY 20

"I am Strong and Successful, because of God."

"Commit to the Lord whatever you do, and your plans will succeed."

PROVERBS 16:3

FOUR PRACTICAL POINTS

- MAKE GOD THE CENTER OF WHAT YOU DO
- BE CONSISTENT IN PRAYER & PRAISE GOD
- ALLOW YOUR PREPARATION TO MEET OPPORTUNITY
- THERE IS A PLAN AND PURPOSE TO LIFE

Understand that God wants nothing more than for you to succeed in life. It is only in his strength that we can accomplish this success in committing our will and plans to him. When things were not clear to me in life, I paused for a reset of strength. It is through his strength, I received in order to raise my three children and nurture my marriage. The power and wisdom of God inspire me to keep moving forward. It was not something I conjured up myself. It was in prayer, fasting, and time with him that he has blessed me. As God had faith in Job; his strength endured. God feels the same towards you and me.

In today's affirmations, we have made a declaration that we are strong because of God. There were apparent times, I did not feel strong. Like, my husband worked as a policeofficer for years. I was always on edge that I would get a call while he was on duty, that he was injured. And when I became overwhelmed and tired, while attending college working a full 8-hour shift, cooking dinner, making a house a home, and assisting my parents in ministry. My strength was gone. Anyone who works will get tired.

Success is not defined by having it "all together". Nor does it mean to have lots of money in the bank. I define my success as lifting my eyes to the hills from whence cometh my help, as Psalms 121 states. I acknowledge that I could not do everything on my own, but with God, I could. The strength of my spirit with inner peace depends on the one who made me strong.

I recognize it was the strength of God in me who made me strong. It was his presence that made my home and marriage successful. Acknowledging this truth has allowed my family and me to make God's name famous through prayer and his word. You can be made strong in the one who has created you.

Set Your Goals

TO ACHIEVING THE PRACTICAL POINTS

GOALS	STEPS
	☐
	☐
POTENTIAL PROBLEMS	☐
	☐
	☐
	☐
STRATEGIES	☐
	☐
	☐

PROGRESS TRACKER

Date	Progress

DAY 21

"It's ok Not to be Ok, because It Will get Better."

"Fear not, for I am with you; be not dismayed, for I am your God; I will strengthen you, help you, and uphold you with my righteous right hand."

ISAIAH 41:10

DAY 21

ED AND ANGEL THE COOPER CHRONICLES PRESENTS...
ANGEL COOPER'S HER CHRONICLES

50 DAYS TO TURNING 50

"Its Ok Not to Be Ok ...cause it'll get Better"

"Allow yourself to Accept your Feelings"

"Accept no Emotion is Permanent"

Fear not, for I am with you; be not dismayed, for I am your God; I will strengthen you, I will help you, I will uphold you with my righteous right hand.
Isaiah 41:10

Get your ebook copy on September 9th.

FOUR PRACTICAL POINTS

- ALLOW YOURSELF TO ACCEPT YOUR FEELINGS
- NO EMOTION IS PERMANENT
- CONFRONT & PROCESS YOUR EMOTIONS
- LEND AN EAR OR SUPPORT THOSE WHO ARE NOT OK

There was a time when I struggled to be the perfect person; mom, wife, friend, and minister. No one told me to set such high standards for myself. I was not ok. I learned through Christ that everything I do will not be perfect. There will be times when the dirty dishes are left in the sink and the laundry may not be washed, folded, and put away. I am ok because I know it will get better.

The enemy will paralyze you with guilt and unhealthy expectations. It is ok not to be ok because it will get better. You do not have to be strong all the time. God is there for you to lean on. Today's affirmation scripture clearly states that in Isaiah 41:10, "fear not for I am with you, be not dismayed for I am your God strengthen you

, help you, and uphold you with my righteous right hand." I love this passage because I realize that there is help and strength for us.

I spoke with God and acknowledged that I was not ok. I was not judged. I began to process what I was feeling during my moments in prayer. My dad would often say if I never had a problem; how would I know God could solve them. Only then, through my circumstances, I realized the power, love, and grace of God.

My sisters gain the courage to lean on God and the strength to move on. It is ok not to be ok. Just do not remain complacent as there is so much for you in life. Do not stay focused on the stuck areas in life. Blaming yourself and others will only make it worse.
Take responsibility for yourself and ask God for help. It causes a release of pain and healing hope to be restored.

Set Your Goals

TO ACHIEVING THE PRACTICAL POINTS

GOALS	STEPS
	☐
	☐
POTENTIAL PROBLEMS	☐
	☐
	☐
	☐
STRATEGIES	☐
	☐
	☐
	☐

PROGRESS TRACKER

Date	Progress

"I am Healed and I Walk in Victory."

"God is our refuge and strength, a very present help in trouble."

PSALMS 46:1

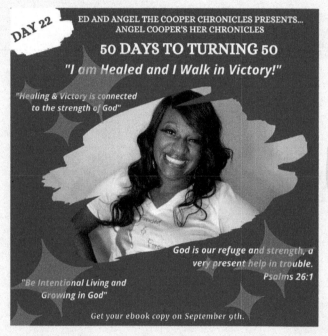

FOUR PRACTICAL POINTS

- HEALING & VICTORY IS CONNECTED TO THE STRENGTH OF GOD
- INTENTIONALLY LIVE AND GROWING IN GOD
- ALLOW HEALING TO TAKE PLACE IN ORDER TO BE MADE WHOLE
- BE CONSISTENT IN QUALITY TIME WITH CHRIST

I was devastated when a doctor told me I would probably never sing again due to voice nodules. Singing is my identity. My dad, who was my pastor, mom, and aunt prayed for me then gave me instructions. I followed those instructions and spoke the promises of God in my life. Today's affirmation, "I am healed and I walk in victory." It is available for anyone who needs healing; physically, emotionally, spiritually, or mentally.

Speaking these words, "I AM HEALED", rejuvenated my spirit after about 6 months. These words were spoken in faith. Understanding faith believes in a person or thing without the need for specific proof or evidence. There was no proof of healing for my voice. when I started my journey of healing, I was highly discouraged. I honestly thought I would never speak again. Let alone sing. I believed the report of my ENT instead of the report of the Lords.

When I shifted my mindset to God wanting me to be healed; everything began to change. In the bible, Job manifested his healing. He decided to trust God and walk in victory. My victory was to come back stronger and better. Even if he did not, I still knew he was able. It is the enemy's job to make you feel discouraged. He is a liar and an accuser of God to make you doubt the promise.

I encourage you to be reminded of the victories on earth and the Bible. God is able. Rest in his power and promise that healing is yours. Do not give up because it is in the moment you want to turn away that your blessing will reveal itself to you. God would be right there wanting to give his healing. There is an old song that says, "he may not come when you want him, but he's always on time." Be strengthened today and walk in your healing victory.

Set Your Goals

TO ACHIEVING THE PRACTICAL POINTS

GOALS	STEPS

POTENTIAL PROBLEMS

STRATEGIES

Steps checkboxes:
- ☐
- ☐
- ☐
- ☐
- ☐
- ☐
- ☐
- ☐
- ☐

PROGRESS TRACKER

Date	Progress

DAY 23

"My Difficult Times are a Part of my Journey. I will Learn to Appreciate my Good."

"Consider it a great joy, my brothers, whenever you experience various trials, knowing that the testing of your faith produces endurance. But endurance must do its complete work so that you may be mature and complete, lacking nothing."

JAMES 1:2-4

ED AND ANGEL THE COOPER CHRONICLES PRESENTS...
ANGEL COOPER'S HER CHRONICLES

50 DAYS TO TURNING 50

DAY 23

Consider it a great joy, my brothers, whenever you experience various trials, knowing that the testing of your faith produces endurance. But endurance must do its complete work, so that you may be mature and complete, lacking nothing.
James 1:2-4

"My Difficult times are apart of my Journey I will learn to appreciate my Good"

"Be aware of your Choices During your Times of Frustration"

"Find someone to talk about your problems"

Get your ebook copy on September 9th.

FOUR PRACTICAL POINTS

- BE AWARE OF YOUR CHOICES DURING YOUR TIMES OF FRUSTRATION
- FIND SOMEONE TO TALK WITH ABOUT YOUR PROBLEMS
- PRACTICE LOOKING ON THE UPSIDE OF THINGS
- IT'S OKAY TO ASK FOR HELP

Life can be challenging. Learning to accept the good and the bad is important. Every part of your journey through life may not be pleasant. It is your experiences that make you. As a believer, it directs us to know the father's strength in prayer. We have referenced Job in the Bible multiple times in this book. After Jobs' difficult times in life, he was blessed. Very similar to the rainbow after a storm.

Today's affirmation helps us to recognize difficult times as a part of the journey. Embracing God through the bad and good allows you to realize trials are a part of our journey. As difficult times arise and the unpleasantness of an abrupt life disruption occurs, evaluate yourself when responding to an issue. Like a text message, if you're angry, don't respond in the heat of the moment. Take your time. Breathe and ask God to give you wisdom at that moment.

So expect difficult times to happen. Similar to boxers entering the ring, prepare yourself to get hit. It is not a surprise as the fighter knows it will happen, just not strictly at the moment. If we prepare or pray daily when difficult times arrive; yes, it will hurt, but God will give us grace for the journey.

Learn to speak to someone if you do not know what to do. Get guidance and prayer for your concerns. Things will get better. The sun will shine again. This too shall pass.

Set Your Goals

TO ACHIEVING THE PRACTICAL POINTS

GOALS	STEPS
	☐
	☐
	☐
POTENTIAL PROBLEMS	☐
	☐
	☐
	☐
STRATEGIES	☐
	☐
	☐

PROGRESS TRACKER

Date	Progress

DAY 24

"I will Show up for Myself because God Shows up for Me."

"The LORD is my light and my salvation— whom shall I fear? The LORD is the strength of my life— of whom shall I be afraid?"

PSALM 27:1

DAY 24

ED AND ANGEL THE COOPER CHRONICLES PRESENTS...
ANGEL COOPER'S HER CHRONICLES

50 DAYS TO TURNING 50

"I will Show up for Myself because God shows up for Me"

"When You are weak God makes us strong. Just call on him."

"When you call God, he will Strengthen you"

FOUR PRACTICAL POINTS

- WHEN YOU ARE WEAK; GOD MAKES US STRONG
- WHEN YOU CALL TO GOD, HE WILL STRENGTHEN YOU
- WHEREVER YOU ARE IN LIFE; GOD IS AVAILABLE TO YOU
- WHOEVER YOU ARE, GOD LOVES YOU

Most of the time, we neglect ourselves. With so many routines in our lives, we wear many hats; boss, entrepreneur, wife, sister, mom, friend, therapist, coach, teacher, aunt, cousin, grandma, minister, and more. At the end of the list is usually left for ourselves. When we consider ourselves, it is an afterthought. By then we are too exhausted to even care.

I appreciate God for constantly reminding us if we make ourselves an afterthought. He graciously reminds me to refuel, reflect, refocus, restore and renew myself. The question is are we listening? The way we show up for everyone else, he desires us to show up on time for ourselves. Today's affirmation is a reminder not to pour from an empty pitcher but gets refilled from Christ. Ways of showing up: acknowledging your worth, appreciating yourself (even if no one else does), accepting that you are good enough, and expressing your gratitude to God for blessing you.

Even Christ took the time to restore himself after he fasted. The enemy tried to attack him at his lowest. The enemy will do the same to you. Remember to show up, look up your Growth & Strength will Go UP.

Set Your Goals

TO ACHIEVING THE PRACTICAL POINTS

GOALS	STEPS
	☐
	☐
POTENTIAL PROBLEMS	☐
	☐
	☐
	☐
STRATEGIES	☐
	☐
	☐
	☐

PROGRESS TRACKER

Date	Progress

DAY 25

"I will Agree with the Great Things that Are for My Life."

"The Lord has done great things for us; we are glad."

PSALM 126:3

ED AND ANGEL THE COOPER CHRONICLES PRESENTS...
ANGEL COOPER'S HER CHRONICLES

50 DAYS TO TURNING 50

The Lord has done great things for us; we are glad.
Psalm 126:3

"I will Align with the "Great Things"

"Be Careful of Negative Thinking"

"Create a Daily Routines"

Get your ebook copy on September 9th.

FOUR PRACTICAL POINTS

- CREATE DAILY ROUTINES
- BE CAREFUL OF NEGATIVE THINKING
- CONSISTENTLY DEVELOP YOUR SKILLS
- CONNECT WITH FRIENDS AND NETWORK

Many times, we can not see the blessings in life because we are too busy begging for more. If we realign our focus and be grateful for the many things that we already have, he will bless us with more. Today's affirmation will encourage us to align ourselves with the great things that happen in our lives.

Sometimes our lives can come out of alignment. Similar to our cars. When the alignment of our car is off when we drive, the car sways to the left or right. This swaying does not give you a smooth car riding experience. The same for our walk with God. If we do not stay in alignment with God our lives will be disrupted. I want to refer to a man in the Bible named Jonah. God gave Jonah an assignment. He refused, so he was swallowed up by a whale.

Read Jonah 3. It was not until Jonah aligned to God's instruction while in the belly of the whale that he was vomited up. He then went forth to do what he was told to do by God.

I want to encourage you to take time to realign and reconnect spiritually with God.

Here are some ways to keep in alignment with God.

- Negative thoughts get us off alignment but reinforcing positive thoughts gets us back in alignment.
- Not praying or reading God's word brings us off alignment.
- Carving out time with God.
- Consider changing your focus. Do not always think of the bad but remember how God brought you through your trial.

Psalms 126;3 says the Lord has done great things for us, and we are glad. Suppose he did an excellent thing for you before he can do it again. Stay in alignment.

Set Your Goals

TO ACHIEVING THE PRACTICAL POINTS

GOALS	STEPS
	☐
	☐
	☐
POTENTIAL PROBLEMS	☐
	☐
	☐
	☐
STRATEGIES	☐
	☐
	☐

PROGRESS TRACKER

Date	Progress

DAY 26

"What I'm Seeking is Coming to Me."

"But seek ye first the kingdom of God, and his righteousness, and all these things shall be added unto you."

MATTHEW 6:33

DAY 26

ED AND ANGEL THE COOPER CHRONICLES PRESENT'S...
ANGEL COOPER'S HER CHRONICLES

50 DAYS TO TURNING 50

"But seek ye first the kingdom of God, and his righteousness; and all these things shall be added unto you."

Matthew 6:33

"When you Seek God... You Learn to Trust his Best for You"

"When you Seek God... Worries don't Consume You"

"WHAT YOU ARE SEEKING ...IS COMING TO YOU"

Get your ebook copy on September 9th.

FOUR PRACTICAL POINTS

- WHEN YOU SEEK GOD; YOU LEARN TO TRUST HIS BEST FOR YOU
- WHEN YOU SEEK GOD; WORRIES DON'T CONSUME YOU
- WHEN YOU SEEK GOD; WE WILL BE STRENGTHENED IN CALLING ON HIM
- WHEN YOU SEEK GOD; YOU RECEIVE BENEFITS OF THE LORD'S BLESSINGS

With my decision to seek God's best for me, I allow myself to receive his best for me. This is how it is done. Intentionally surrendering desires, ideas, and dreams for the kingdom to use. You shall be blessed. In today's affirmation, "what I am seeking" comes directly from seeking God.

In seeking God, I have to consider what God wants for me. What should I do to pursue the will of God? When I seek his kingdom, the kingdom of God is where God reigns supreme. Jesus Christ is Lord and King. Having the heart to seek after God's kingdom does not mean you're blameless. It means you're intentionally getting it right. Read about King David 1 Samuel 13:14. It is about returning to God after seeking repentance and forgiveness.

The concept of a kingdom is not one of space, territory but rather one of kingly rule in sovereign control. I seek God's direction for my life. When in prayer and devotion, It is realized we wouldn't see his things for our lives. We always feel inadequate & insufficient. Those he called he qualified.

In remembering in kingdom assignments, we walk by faith, not by sight. Noah didn't see the rain; he followed instructions to build the boat according to God's word. Everything will align itself when you're obedient to kingdom work.

I encourage you to seek God earnestly in prayer in fasting for guidance.
Trust him even when you can't trace him. When it's a kingdom assignment, you will face troubles and persecution but keep the faith. In every trial, if God brings you to it, he will get you through it. When you call on Christ seeking strength, God will show up for you.

Set Your Goals

TO ACHIEVING THE PRACTICAL POINTS

GOALS	STEPS
	☐
	☐
	☐
POTENTIAL PROBLEMS	☐
	☐
	☐
STRATEGIES	☐
	☐
	☐
	☐

PROGRESS TRACKER

Date	Progress

DAY 27

"God is Giving me Strength For My Struggle."

"God is our refuge and strength, a very present help in trouble."

PSALM 46:1

FOUR PRACTICAL POINTS

- STRENGTH AND POWER IS PROMISED
- STRENGTHENED YOURSELF BY THE POSITIVITY OF MUSIC, PRAYER & WORSHIP
- SURROUND YOURSELF WITH PEOPLE WHO APPRECIATE YOUR WORTH
- MEDITATE AND READ GOD'S WORD FOR STRENGTH

When faced with struggles, it is hard to see the good in anything you are doing. Understanding where your source of strength comes from will allow you to gain.

There is a blueprint God clearly states in Psalms 46:1 God is our refuge and strength, a very present help in trouble. If we require the power of shelter, we can ask God. If we need help during trouble, we can ask God. The problem is, are we asking God for help?

Struggles are defined as forceful or violent efforts to get free of restraint or constriction.

Each struggle is uniquely designed with the same result in mind. A distraction to keep you off course in achieving the original goal set forth. Not allowing this struggle to distract you is the fight. In Christ, God provides help and successful outcomes when we trust in him. I can't help but think of Daniel in Lion's den, a famous story in the Bible. King Darius' friends to Daniel developed a vicious plot to have him thrown into the den because of his faith. In his struggle, it became apparent God was no match for the lions or any battle. Daniel came out stronger and with the victory. Daniel 6.

Strength is promised when we ask God for assistance. The issue is looking in the wrong direction for help and why we are not achieving our goal. Today, during this affirmation, I pray that you recognize Jesus is our help, and if we need him, he is right there for us. I want to take advantage of the strategies of prayer, fasting, reading the word, and reaffirming the promises of God over your life.

In trusting God through the struggles, I know that it is not the end. It is the beginning of an incredible journey God has for you if you believe. Protect your peace, create your boundaries. Know that God promises never to leave you or forsake you.

Set Your Goals

TO ACHIEVING THE PRACTICAL POINTS

GOALS	STEPS
	☐
	☐
	☐
POTENTIAL PROBLEMS	☐
	☐
	☐
	☐
STRATEGIES	☐
	☐
	☐

PROGRESS TRACKER

Date	Progress

DAY 28

"It is Ok to Say, No."

"And I sent messengers unto them, saying, I am doing great work, so that I cannot come down: why should the work cease, while I leave it, and come down to you?"

NEHEMIAH 6:3

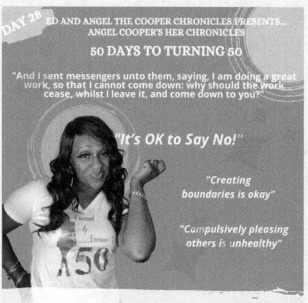

Get your ebook copy on September 9th.

FOUR PRACTICAL POINTS

- CREATING BOUNDARIES IS OK
- YOU CANNOT POUR FROM AN EMPTY CUP; TAKE CARE OF YOU
- COMPULSIVELY PLEASING OTHERS IS UNHEALTHY
- CONFIDENTLY KNOW YOU ARE AMAZING

In showing up for everyone, have you learned to say "No," not this time? It is all right to say no. One of the smallest yet most powerful words used in the entire world is "no." It is a difficult task, always trying to please people. It drains you physically and mentally and takes time away from spending it with the ones you love. Today's affirmation permits you to protect your joy, peace, and time.

When you're continuously accepting obligations in saying yes, you never have time to evaluate the most important treasures in life. Being challenged to reach your potential means you'll never achieve the fruition or fullness in life because your focus is off. You cannot see the bigger picture because you are constantly trying to please others.

When you get an opportunity, read Nehemiah 1. In this chapter, you will read about a man given an assignment. Do you see the correlation? Nehemiah was instructed to rebuild a wall to keep out the villains and secure the city. People heard of this great work he was doing and came to distract him. After conspiring multiple times to get Nehemiah to come off the wall, he responded by simply saying "no". He said, "I'm doing great work, I can't come down. (Nehemiah 6). Recognize the distractions in your life. Remain focused and be ready to say no in order to continue your assignment or work.

Romans 8:31
King James Version31 What shall we then say to these things? If God is for us, who can be against us?

Set Your Goals

TO ACHIEVING THE PRACTICAL POINTS

GOALS	STEPS
	☐

POTENTIAL PROBLEMS

STRATEGIES

PROGRESS TRACKER

Date	Progress

<u>"I will Remember that the Difficult Times are Temporary."</u>

"For I consider that the sufferings of this present time are not worth comparing with the glory that is to be revealed to us."

ROMANS 8:18 6:3

ED AND ANGEL THE COOPER CHRONICLES PRESENTS...
ANGEL COOPER'S HER CHRONICLES

50 DAYS TO TURNING 50

" *I will Remember that the Difficult times are Temporary.*"

For I consider that the sufferings of this present time are not worth comparing with the glory that is to be revealed to us.

"Talk about the difficulty."

"Try to See Past the Difficulties"

Get your ebook copy on September 9th.

FOUR PRACTICAL POINTS

- TALK ABOUT THE DIFFICULTY
- TRY TO SEE PAST THE DIFFICULTIES
- ASK FOR HELP THROUGH THE DIFFICULTY
- AM I EXPERIENCING A CATASTROPHE OR DIFFICULT INCONVENIENCE?

"Success isn't permanent,& failure isn't fatal, it's the courage to continue that counts."-Mike Ditka. This book of affirmations is a reminder of the goodness of God during difficult times. God is with you. My assignment is to encourage and empower you. I am here to declare the kingdom of God is at hand and we have no time to give up now.

Remember earlier we talked about Lot's wife? Please read Luke 17:32. The scripture says, "Remember Lot's wife." That's it. Why that verse and just those words? Because there is no time in saying you will trust God, yet when he says move forward, you turn to allow your circumstances to confine you. He knows that these moments are fleeting and temporary. He has chosen you, he'll strengthen for the call.

We do not deny that the difficult time is real with the pressure mounting every day. Our scripture Romans 8:18 says it best to consider that the sufferings of this present time are not worth comparing with the glory that has to be revealed in us.

I want to remind you that your current condition is temporary. The sun will shine again. Glory comes after the struggle. The sun comes after the rain. Whatever you are being challenged consider there will be glory after, keyword after, you go through as God will reveal his strength.

TODAY'S AFFIRMATION & DECLARATION

Set Your Goals

TO ACHIEVING THE PRACTICAL POINTS

GOALS	STEPS

☐
☐
☐
☐
☐
☐
☐
☐
☐
☐

POTENTIAL PROBLEMS

STRATEGIES

PROGRESS TRACKER

Date	Progress

DAY 30

"Every Day is a Step Toward Improvement and Healing."

"And my God will meet all your needs according to the riches of his glory in Christ Jesus."

PHILIPPIANS 4:19

FOUR PRACTICAL POINTS

- ASK GOD FOR WISDOM
- PRACTICE SELF-COMPASSION
- APPRECIATE THE POSITIVE
- DISPLAY KINDNESS GESTURES

I challenged myself to change my diet to ultimately improve my health. I know it is going to be a challenge but I will take a step in the right direction of living a healthy lifestyle. I had given myself a deadline with no grace for this journey. It took time to load the pounds on, so it will take some time to trim them off. My fitness trainer was awesome at helping me to see this. She created a daily schedule or routine for me to follow. Eventually, with accountability, I'll reach my goal.

If you desire to make effective change, you need to start somewhere. Create a plan. The Bible says to write the vision and make it plain. Every step you make is closer to achieving your goal. There is a quote I love. I am not sure who wrote it, but the author says,"it is better to take many small steps in the right direction than to make a great leap forward only to stumble backward.

One of my first approaches to a healthier life was changing my mindset when it comes to my meals; the preparation and how I want to feel after eating. The mind is your biggest battleground. Once you make up your mind, it gets easier.

Every step that I take brings me closer to my finish line. No, I'm not there yet, but I am not where I used to be. Rest, but don't quit. Keep going. Challenging situations build tough people. Start where you are. Use what you have. Do what you can. - Arthur Ashe.

TODAY'S AFFIRMATION & DECLARATION

Set Your Goals

TO ACHIEVING THE PRACTICAL POINTS

GOALS	STEPS

POTENTIAL PROBLEMS

STRATEGIES

- ☐
- ☐
- ☐
- ☐
- ☐
- ☐
- ☐
- ☐
- ☐

PROGRESS TRACKER

Date	Progress

DAY 31

<u>"I'm Releasing my Past and Pressing Towards my Future."</u>

"I press toward the mark for the prize of the high calling of God in Christ Jesus."

PHILIPPIANS 3:14

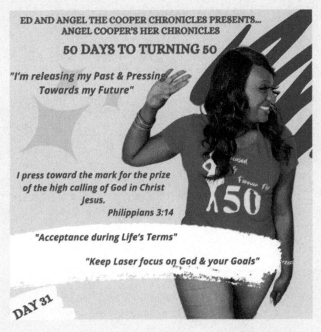

<u>FOUR PRACTICAL POINTS</u>

- ACCEPTANCE DURING LIFE'S TERMS
- KEEP LASER FOCUS ON GOD & YOUR GOALS
- PRACTICE AN ATTITUDE OF GRATITUDE
- TAKE TIME TO RENEW YOURSELF

I am making room for my blessings. I'm sure you're doing the same. I decided I no longer would sit around waiting or delaying what God had given me to do. Then I recognized what was holding me back. My past fear and inadequacies always remind me I was not good enough or qualified enough for the assignment. The acronym for fear is false, evidence, appearing, natural. I no longer became a victim of my past and decided to release the past and press forward to my bright future.

Today's affirmation and scripture were on repeat for me during my most difficult times. Philippians 3:14 says, "I press toward the mark for the prize of the high calling of God in Christ Jesus."I have begun to understand and embrace my current prayer; on GodI did get disappointedwhen I did not reach my desired goal, but I kept on pressing. I can genuinely say I am not where I want to be, but I'm not where I used to be because of my press.

Paul in the Bible speaks of this press. Due to the trial, there was no possible way to handle it on his own. As we are all faced with trials, be like Apostle Paul. The Bible says, I see you, and you're doing a good job. In the middle of the fight, I implore you not to walk away but press towards God for Strength, Peace, Wisdom, and Guidance.

Set Your Goals

TO ACHIEVING THE PRACTICAL POINTS

GOALS	STEPS
	☐
	☐
POTENTIAL PROBLEMS	☐
	☐
	☐
	☐
STRATEGIES	☐
	☐
	☐
	☐

PROGRESS TRACKER

Date	Progress

DAY 32

"I am in the Process of Becoming the Best Version of Myself."

"Therefore, if anyone is in Christ, he is a new creation; old things have passed away; behold, all things have become new."

2 CORINTHIANS 5:17

FOUR PRACTICAL POINTS

- SHOW UP FOR YOURSELF
- DON'T SWEAT THE SMALL STUFF
- DO THE WORK NO SHORTCUTS
- ASK FOR HELP

I want you to get into the habit of believing and encouraging yourself because you are becoming the best version of yourself. It is easy to align your thoughts with a foundational word when you know your God's creation; wonderfully and beautifully made. Clear out anything and everything that people have said to you and replace it with God's thoughts of you.

Today's affirmation challenges us to approach the process with openness. No one appreciates the process of progress, advance in the process of time: something going on: proceeding. Before you get there, there are a series of events happening. In our scripture today, 2 Corinthians 5:17 "therefore if anyone is in Christ, he is a creation.

Old things have passed away; behold, all things have become new".

We often do not believe our old past or thoughts can be put away or let go. I am here to tell you in Christ you are made new. The word process requires you to be present going through with an openness of becoming your best self. When you are willing and ready, it is all you need. God's guidance and growth will meet you with a new sense of confidence in Christ.

Set Your Goals

TO ACHIEVING THE PRACTICAL POINTS

GOALS	STEPS
	☐
	☐
POTENTIAL PROBLEMS	☐
	☐
	☐
	☐
STRATEGIES	☐
	☐
	☐
	☐

PROGRESS TRACKER

Date	Progress

DAY 33

"I Thank God I Did not Give up on Myself."

"Now unto Him who can do exceedingly abundantly above all that we ask or think, according to the power that works in us."

EPHESIANS 3:20

FOUR PRACTICAL POINTS

- CREATE A HEALTHY ROUTINE
- DON'T ALLOW EXCUSES TO STOP YOU
- CELEBRATE SMALL VICTORIES
- BE ACCOUNTABLE TO YOURSELF AND OTHERS

A few scriptures were on repeat to help me in my most challenging times in life. This was one of the scripture I would say while driving with tears running down my face. I knew God would do it, although it had not manifested itself in my life. I wanted our children to be settled in life and self-sufficient. I wanted healing in my marriage, a successful ministry, and business. I believe that God could exceed my expectations, but it was taking too long.

I was not acknowledging the small achievements in my children's lives or recognizing the small steps Ed, my husband was making in our marriage in order for us to grow stronger. I almost gave up, but I thank God for opening me to see working within us even in small things. Today's affirmation is tothank

God that I (you) did not give up on myself (oneself). For me, I was grateful for not giving up in year twelve, fourteen, or fifteen of this twenty-nine-year marriage. There was so much in store on the other side of our pain and pressure. The enemy's job is to make us give up. Believing it is not worth fighting for. Let me say to you; you are worth the fight. As well as your marriage, family, and children. The darkest hour is just before the light of day, so do not give up on yourself; there is so much in store if you go through.

Set Your Goals

TO ACHIEVING THE PRACTICAL POINTS

GOALS	STEPS
	☐
	☐
POTENTIAL PROBLEMS	☐
	☐
	☐
	☐
STRATEGIES	☐
	☐
	☐
	☐

PROGRESS TRACKER

Date	Progress

DAY 34

"I'm so Glad that Trouble Won't Last Always."

"Do not let your hearts be troubled. You believe in God and also believe in me."

JOHN 14:1

FOUR PRACTICAL POINTS

- REMAIN LASER-FOCUSED ON GOD & HIS PLAN FOR YOU
- HAVE AN OPENNESS FOR INSTRUCTION OR GUIDANCE
- CHOOSE TO LIVE COURAGEOUSLY OR BE CONTENTIOUS
- SURRENDER TO GOD TO BRING YOU THROUGH

The truth of the matter is once you are finished with one troubled moment, another one is right around the corner. There is a scripture that reminds us that there is trouble on every side, yet not distressed; we are perplexed, but not in despair; persecuted, but not forsaken; cast down, but not destroyed. I need you to be encouraged; even though you are going through a storm right now. God has not forgotten about you.

I want to bring to your attention a man in the Bible by the name of Joseph. His story is found in Genesis 39. Joseph went from one storm to the next or one troubling moment to the next. From the pit to the palace and to the prison and then the fulfillment of the promise. Joseph went through many different phases of ongoing difficulty. It seemed his problems would never end. Let's map out his story.

- From being thrown into the pit by his brothers, who were jealous of him.
- While Joseph was working in the palace, the king's wife lied that he assaulted her.
- He was then thrown into prison. He was rescued by one of the king's men passing by the pit, which then sold & brought him to Egypt.
- While in prison, Joseph interpreted a dream for the baker and butler. Once the butler was released, the king needed an interpreter for his dream; the butler remembered joseph.
- Joseph shared the interpretation with the king.
- The interpretation came true and all were prepared for the famine.
- The king set him up as a leader because of the interpretation.
- When His brothers showed up to see the king in order to get assistance during the famine, they had to address Joseph and not recognize their brother.

His troubles seem to be ongoing, but they did not last. There is an expiration date for your problems. Joseph endured and trusted God through it all. As with the story of Joseph, I do not have a day or time when your trouble will end, but rest assured, I promise you trouble does not always last. There is always something to learn from our problems. It builds strength, endurance, and powerful prayer life.

Set Your Goals

TO ACHIEVING THE PRACTICAL POINTS

GOALS	STEPS
	☐
	☐
POTENTIAL PROBLEMS	☐
	☐
	☐
	☐
STRATEGIES	☐
	☐
	☐

PROGRESS TRACKER

Date	Progress

DAY 35

"I Trust and Know Eventually Everything will be All Right."

"Trust in the Lord with all thine heart; and lean not unto thine own understanding. In all thy ways acknowledge him, and he shall direct thy paths."

PROVERBS 3:5-6

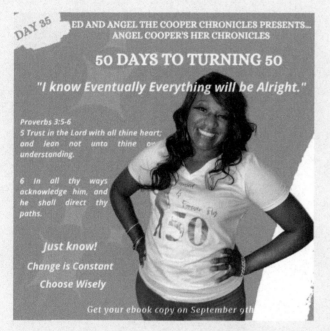

FOUR PRACTICAL POINTS

- CHANGE IS CONSTANT
- CHOOSE WISELY
- LOOK TO THE FUTURE, NOT JUST THE MOMENT
- FOCUS ON WHAT YOU CAN CONTROL ANYTHING ELSE LEAVE IT ALONE

There is a quote that I love and want to share with you. "Don't panic, everything is going to be alright, trust God and let him work"--unknown. It is tough for us to allow God to do his perfect work without our interference. It usually turns out better when God is in charge, anyway. I suggest that you get out of the way and let him do what he does best.

Today's affirmation is trusting and knowing, eventually everything will be all right. Learn to let go and let God have your problems. Part of you wants to let go, but your mind wants to know how it will be resolved. Your mind or your carnal self does not know how God will show up for you which complicates your trust. Trust is not tangible, so you do not see trust or feel confident. You have in God to do the impossible.

The scripture for today is Proverbs 3:5-6. "Trust in the Lord with all thine heart, and lean not unto thine own understanding. In all thy ways acknowledge him, and he shall direct thy paths". A good example of trusting in God is the story of Joseph. No matter how long it takes, from the pit to the palace or the prison and to the palace again. Don't give up on God because he won't give up on you.

Set Your Goals

TO ACHIEVING THE PRACTICAL POINTS

GOALS	STEPS
	☐
	☐
POTENTIAL PROBLEMS	☐
	☐
	☐
STRATEGIES	☐
	☐
	☐
	☐
	☐

PROGRESS TRACKER

Date	Progress

DAY 36

"I May have Made a Mistake, but I am Not a Mistake."

"And be ye kind one to another, tenderhearted, forgiving one another, even as God for Christ's sake hath forgiven you."

EPHESIANS 4:32

DAY 36

ED AND ANGEL THE COOPER CHRONICLES PRESENTS...
ANGEL COOPER'S HER CHRONICLES

50 DAYS TO TURNING 50

"I May have Made a Mistake, but I am Not a Mistake."

But you,Lord, are a compassionate and graciousGod, slow to anger,abounding in love and faithfulness.16 Turn to me and have mercy on me; show your strength in behalf of your servant; save me, because I serve you just as my mother did.

Psalm 86:15-16

Admittance to it & Acceptance of it

FOUR PRACTICAL POINTS

- ADMITTANCE TO IT & ACCEPTANCE OF IT
- REGARD IT AS A LESSON LEARNED
- FORGIVE YOURSELF
- STOP & DON'T DO IT AGAIN

When it comes to making mistakes, it is acknowledging you have made a mistake and owning it. But listen, don't become it. No one is immune or exempt from making mistakes. We all make them. It is how you respond. It is like my dad always said, it is ten percent of what happens to you but ninety percent of how you respond? News flash is not the end of the world. If you make a mistake, you can learn from it. It takes courage to admit that you did something wrong. It takes even more courage to make the necessary corrections.

In college, I took a class called "Reframing Failure". The class taught me how to approach failure differently. Not ignoring failure, but looking at it as a lesson learned. This concept definitely resets your mind; approaching everything with a willingness to be open to constructive criticism and improvements.

Today affirms that I may have made a mistake, but I am not a mistake. Whatever you do remember, we all have made poor choices, but it is okay. You live and you learn.
Be honest in evaluating the process of the mistake. Think of Jonah, while in the belly of the whale, he had time to admit that he was wrong for disobeying God. Once the whale vomited Jonah up, he decided to move forward. I am sure Jonah did not want to relive that mistake.

As we always are quick to forgive others; remember to give yourself some compassion and grace as we all make mistakes. Learn and grow from them. Our scripture is a reminder, so allow this to strengthen you. "And be ye kind one to another, tenderhearted, forgiving one another, even as God for Christ's sake hath forgiven you."
Ephesians 4:32

Set Your Goals

TO ACHIEVING THE PRACTICAL POINTS

GOALS	STEPS
	☐
	☐
	☐

POTENTIAL PROBLEMS

☐
☐
☐
☐

STRATEGIES

☐
☐
☐

PROGRESS TRACKER

Date	Progress

"I will be Patient with Myself as God is Not Through with Me Yet."

"Being confident that he who began a good work in you will carry it on to completion until the day of Christ Jesus.

PHILIPPIANS 1:6

FOUR PRACTICAL POINTS

- WAIT IN EXPECTATION
- WAIT IN THE POWER OF PRAYER
- WAIT ON GOD'S TIMING
- WAIT IN STRENGTH

What do you do while you are waiting on your blessing? What do you do while you are becoming your best self? Most of us do not have patience like Job in the Bible. We are not willing to endure the problem. Today's affirmation, "I will be patient with myself as God is not through with me".

The word patience is defined as the quality or virtue of patience is presented as either forbearance or endurance. In the former sense, it is a quality of self-restraint or of not giving way to anger, even in the face of provocation; it is attributed to both God and man and is closely related to mercy and compassion. Why we don't have the endurance for ourselves is mindblowing. We will wait for everything or everyone else, and weimmediately dismissourselves. Today that changes, We declare and decree we will have God's patience over our life because God is not through with me yet.

Our friend, Job, is the greatest illustration of patience. We may have heard the saying. I have the patience of Job, are you sure? I mean, even his wife said, "curse God and die". Regardless of our length of time of suffering, we are called to use Job as an example. Endure with strength, endure with faith and endure with patience. God is bringing you out like Job; stronger, better, and wiser.

Set Your Goals

TO ACHIEVING THE PRACTICAL POINTS

GOALS	STEPS
	☐

POTENTIAL PROBLEMS

STRATEGIES

PROGRESS TRACKER

Date	Progress

DAY 38

"I May Not Be Where I Want to Be, but I'm Not Where I Used to Be."

"Being confident that he who began a good work in you will carry it on to completion until the day of Christ Jesus."

PHILIPPIANS 1:6

ED AND ANGEL THE COOPER CHRONICLES PRESENTS...
ANGEL COOPER'S HER CHRONICLES

50 DAYS TO TURNING 50

"I May not be Where I Want to be but I'm Not Where I Used to Be."

"Brethren, I count not myself to have apprehended: but this one thing I do, forgetting those things which are behind, and reaching forth unto those things which are before."

Philippians 3:13

Tips.....
Reset your Mindset
Reevaluate your Goals

FOUR PRACTICAL POINTS

- WAIT IN EXPECTATION
- WAIT IN THE POWER OF PRAYER
- WAIT ON GOD'S TIMING
- WAIT IN STRENGTH

What do you do while you are waiting on your blessing? What do you do while you are becoming your best self? Most of us do not have patience like Job in the Bible. We are not willing to endure the problem. Today's affirmation, "I will be patient with myself as God is not through with me".

The word patience is defined as the quality or virtue of patience is presented as either forbearance or endurance. In the former sense, it is a quality of self-restraint or of not giving way to anger, even in the face of provocation; it is attributed to both God and man and is closely related to mercy and compassion. Why we don't have the endurance for ourselves is mindblowing. We will wait for everything or everyone else, and we immediately dismiss ourselves. Today that changes, We declare and decree we will have God's patience over our life because God is not through with me yet.

Our friend, Job, is the greatest illustration of patience. We may have heard the saying. I have the patience of Job, are you sure? I mean, even his wife said, "curse God and die". Regardless of our length of time of suffering, we are called to use Job as an example. Endure with strength, endure with faith and endure with patience. God is bringing you out like Job; stronger, better, and wiser.

Set Your Goals

TO ACHIEVING THE PRACTICAL POINTS

GOALS	STEPS
	☐
	☐
POTENTIAL PROBLEMS	☐
	☐
	☐
	☐
STRATEGIES	☐
	☐
	☐

PROGRESS TRACKER

Date	Progress

DAY 39

"My Faith is Stronger Than My Fear."

"So that we may boldly say, The Lord is my helper, and I will not fear what man shall do unto me."

HEBREWS 13:6

FOUR PRACTICAL POINTS

- DEAL WITH THE FEAR; DON'T IGNORE IT
- DISCOVER CREATIVE WAYS TO COMBAT FEAR
- DON'T ALLOW FEAR TO INFLUENCE YOU TO ALLOW GOD
- DAILY CHOOSE TO WALK BOLDLY WITH GOD, NOT FEAR

Challenging and uncertain times can be really scary, but each day I want you to decide, boldly, "my faith is stronger than my fear and I will live in faith".

What is faith? Faith is the complete trust or confidence in someone or something. What is fear? Fear is an unpleasant emotion caused by a belief that someone or something is dangerous. I guarantee that you have all that it takes to exercise this God-given notion and message.

Today's affirmation will remind us that you have it within you to achieve great things. When I decided to start my health and wellness improvement journey, I knew it would take some time to lose weight does not happen overnight. I had to remind myself. It takes time and effort. I had to be willing to put in the time. I am allowing my faith to supersede my fear of failing in this area.

The biggest mistake I encountered was when I cheated on my diet and ate the wrong foods. I refused to stay down. I got back up and tried again until it became second nature to me. I prayed and asked God for strength. Then I began putting in the work of shopping and preparing foods to be ready when the cravings hit. When I had the right types of food in the place, it became easier for me.

Understanding this concept of "I can with a plan." Fear had me in its grip until I realized food did not control me. I have it under my control. My faith is bigger than my fear, and I will achieve everything I set out to do.

TODAY'S AFFIRMATION & DECLARATION

Set Your Goals

TO ACHIEVING THE PRACTICAL POINTS

GOALS	STEPS

GOALS

POTENTIAL PROBLEMS

STRATEGIES

STEPS

☐
☐
☐
☐
☐
☐
☐
☐
☐
☐

PROGRESS TRACKER

Date	Progress

DAY 40

<u>"I am Brave, Bold, and Blessed."</u>

"Fear thou not, for I am with thee; be not dismayed, for I am thy God; I will strengthen thee; yea, I will help thee; yea, I will uphold thee with the right hand of my righteousness."

ISAIAH 41:10

FOUR PRACTICAL POINTS

- BELIEVE & ACTIVELY SEEK OUT THE BLESSINGS IN LIFE
- BELIEVE IN GOD ALL THINGS ARE POSSIBLE
- BELIEVE DAILY STRENGTH OF GOD WILL EMPOWER YOU
- BELIEVE THE PRESENCE OF GOD WILL BE WITH YOU

I want to show you how to process the concept of being brave, bold, and blessed. It is only through Christ as he will empower you with everything you need only if you depend on him. Brave means that you are ready to face and endure danger or pain. You show courage. Bold means that you show an ability to take risks, confidence, and courage. Blessed means that you are made holy; consecrated. In today's affirmation, I proclaim that I am Brave, Bold, and Blessed.

It is possible that even the quietest person can become bold and brave. When you begin to operate with Christ boldly and bravely, God gives a certain grace to walk with authority. Allowing Christ to lead and guide you makes the difference. As Christ displayed his boldness by to the cross and completing his mission for God. Know that you share the same characteristics in your assignment.

Would you please not allow the enemy to trick you out of your blessings because you refused to walk bravely or stand boldly? David walked boldly to kill the giant Goliath. Even though David was the underdog, he chose to walk boldly with God and to stand and be brave. Allow this story and lesson to encourage you in the success of being brave and bold. Success is evident. You will always remain blessed.

Set Your Goals

TO ACHIEVING THE PRACTICAL POINTS

GOALS	STEPS
	☐
	☐
POTENTIAL PROBLEMS	☐
	☐
	☐
	☐
STRATEGIES	☐
	☐
	☐

PROGRESS TRACKER

Date	Progress

<u>ABC's of Affirmation...</u>
<u>I am AMAZING, BRILLIANT & COURAGEOUS</u>

"Be strong and courageous. Do not be afraid or terrified because of them, for the Lord your God goes with you; he will never leave you nor forsake you."

PHILIPPIANS 1:6

FOUR PRACTICAL POINTS

- BE A LIFELONG LEARNER
- BE AUTHENTICALLY YOU
- RECOGNIZE HAVING HEALTHY PERSPECTIVE
- REALIZE TAKING HEALTHY RISKS ARE BENEFICIAL

My mission is to inspire others with God's word offering confidence and promise. We need to be reminded of how Christ sees us while going through situations. The Bible is filled with God's overcoming power. There is no better way than to use the ABCs of affirmation to reaffirm his love for us. In today's affirmation, "I am Amazing, Brilliant, and Courageous". The affirmation starts with the first three letters of the alphabet to empower us to live in full expectation of God's plan for our life.

Replace the negative thoughts with his truths about whom God says you are. God comforts, strengthens, and inspires his believers to see us the way he sees us. An affirmation helps you create your reality, structures your worldview, and confirms your beliefs. Do you know how God sees you? I encourage you to change the way you see yourself. You are the healed and blessed of God.

In Job's life, he had to speak and reaffirm the reality of who he was in God. Not looking at his current condition and what he was experiencing. He had to block out the negativity of his wife and friends to remember what God had promised him. And in the end, he was victorious. Words shape and frame our world. Once the words are spoken out, it begins to materialize. Begin the transformation of reaffirming what has been already spoken. We are dispelling our insecurities in exchange for God's plan for our lives. Walk tall and bold in these affirmations; it will change your life completely.

Set Your Goals

TO ACHIEVING THE PRACTICAL POINTS

GOALS	STEPS
	☐
	☐
	☐
POTENTIAL PROBLEMS	☐
	☐
	☐
	☐
STRATEGIES	☐
	☐
	☐

PROGRESS TRACKER

Date	Progress

"I have Limitless Potential in Christ."

"But He said, "All things that are impossible with people are possible with God."

PHILIPPIANS 1:6

FOUR PRACTICAL POINTS

- SET SHORT & LONG TERM GOALS
- SPEND YOUR TIME WISELY
- REMAIN POSITIVE IN GOD & KEEP OUT NEGATIVITY
- RECHARGE & REST TO REACH YOUR FULLEST POTENTIAL

When you become a believer of the word of God, you obtain a divine power to operate and function in him. The Holy Spirit is the limitless divine power of potential that works in and for you. Once you realize it is the source of your strength, Luke 18:27 becomes alive. "All things are possible with God." There is another passage of scripture that says, "not that we are sufficient of ourselves to think anything as of ourselves, but our sufficiency is of God (2 Corinthians 3:5).

You realize that I am nothing without God on my side. God's all-sufficiency is that nothing else needs to be revealed for God's plan for us. It is a completely done deal. Confidently in your potential, you can refuse to bow to the spirit of intimidation, fear, and hopelessness. With Christ at the center, anything can be obtainable and possible to them that believe. The question is- do you think that God can and will do exceeding and abundantly above all you can ask or think.

Now, the challenge is to allow yourself to reach your full potential by having or showing the capacity to become or develop into something in the future. God's plan for us is to succeed and thrive. With our free will to choose, I pray that you decide potential in Christ, which is his best for you in being everything the father in heaven has designed.

Set Your Goals

TO ACHIEVING THE PRACTICAL POINTS

GOALS	STEPS
	☐
	☐
POTENTIAL PROBLEMS	☐
	☐
	☐
	☐
STRATEGIES	☐
	☐
	☐

PROGRESS TRACKER

Date	Progress

<u>"I Don't Just Live for Things; I Live to Fulfill my Purpose."</u>

"

"And we know that for those who love God, all things work together for good, for those who are called according to His purpose."

ROMANS 8:28 ESV

FOUR PRACTICAL POINTS

- LEARN TO PURSUE YOUR PASSION
- LOOK AT THE BIGGER PICTURE
- LIVE ON PURPOSE
- LISTEN TO GUIDANCE FROM GOD

It is important to take the time and reflect on what fuels and moves you in life. Some may call it purpose or destiny; others may call it a realization or an awakening to your reason of existence. How you spend your time doing what makes you happy or giving your time in a positive way matters. Living just materialistically is fleeting. It dissolves and goes away quickly. Learn to establish a lifelong effect on what you positively foster in fulfilling your purpose.

Do not just live for cars, money, houses, or things; live purposefully. Today's affirmation encourages you to ask God what your proposed design is. Find out why you are here and what you should be doing with your life. Using this book in prayer, fasting and seeking God's word. Over, he will begin to make it plain and clear.

Find your mission in order to please God. Commit to learning and living on purpose. Our scripture is clear today Romans 8:28 ESV, "And we know that for those who love God, all things work together for good, for those who are called according to his purpose".

Set Your Goals

TO ACHIEVING THE PRACTICAL POINTS

GOALS	STEPS
	☐
	☐
POTENTIAL PROBLEMS	☐
	☐
	☐
	☐
STRATEGIES	☐
	☐
	☐
	☐

PROGRESS TRACKER

Date	Progress

DAY 44

"I Permit Me to Be Great."

"And whatever you ask in prayer, you will receive if you have faith."

PHILIPPIANS 1:6

FOUR PRACTICAL POINTS

- DEFINE YOUR MORALS & VALUES
- PREPARE FOR THE PROCESS
- PRACTICE LOVING YOURSELF & OTHERS
- DECIDE TO REMAIN CONFIDENT & COURAGEOUS

My husband and I coined this statement, "Love is Worth the Work", when we would go live on social media to inspire others in relationships. One of the reasons we began having this desire to speak this way was because of our children. We told them they could not be average whatever they do in life. "Go at it150%". One of my coaches' statements that she shared with my group was, "how you do anything is how you do everything."

Permitting oneself is this; when you let go of what you think will happen, you allow yourself to see what happens, and that openness and self-trust can unlock so many doors. In today's affirmation, if you are holding back at being everything God has for you to be, this is the moment to release your preconceived notion, step forwardand pursue.

The scripture in Matthew 21:22 provides some insight,"And whatever you ask in prayer, you will receive, if you have faith". We encourage you to activate your faith, having no fear, and permit yourself to be great. Allow yourself self-care Saturday and a fabulous Friday in order for you to shine bright for the world to see Christ at work in you. Release and let go! God permits you to be great!

Set Your Goals

TO ACHIEVING THE PRACTICAL POINTS

GOALS	STEPS
	☐
	☐
POTENTIAL PROBLEMS	☐
	☐
	☐
	☐
STRATEGIES	☐
	☐
	☐

PROGRESS TRACKER

Date	Progress

DAY 45

<u>"I'm Becoming What God has For Me</u>
<u>to be Every Day."</u>

"And do not be conformed to this world, but be transformed by the renewing of your mind, so that you may prove what the will of God is, that which is good and acceptable and perfect."

PHILIPPIANS 1:6

FOUR PRACTICAL POINTS

- STAND WITH INTEGRITY IN GOD
- STAND WITH OBEDIENCE TO GOD
- STAND IN BOLDNESS WITH GOD
- STAND IN PRAYER TO GOD

One of my all-time favorite scriptures and books in the Bible is Proverbs 3:5 and 6 and Romans 12:2. It gives a layout on how to renew your way and mind. When I was a young Christian, I wanted to understand how to have a great relationship with God that everyone talked about. This verse enlightened me to begin the walk with God. Romans 12:2, "and do not be conformed to this world, but be transformed by the renewing of your mind, so that you may prove what the will of God is, that which is good and acceptable and perfect". This was a first-hand step in practical ways and strategies in Becoming You in God...

What does your mind think about your situation? Do you have stinking thinking? It is time to renew, refocus or reset your mind. Give yourself some grace as you are in the transition of becoming whom you are meant to be. The word "becoming'' is the process of coming to be something or of passing into a state. In 2018, former First Lady Michelle Obama wrote her book "Becoming". One because she's beautiful inside and out. It embraces both the highs and lows of life.

Everything that you have endured throughout life has led you to "becoming" who you are today. Along the way, you have experienced pitfalls and roadblocks. Flush out the negative thoughts; educate, enhance and develop every area in your life. Renewing your mind daily with the word of God will help you on your way to greatness. Challenge yourself to reach your fullest potential. God loves you. Understanding how God sees you, ultimately, is all that matters to "becoming" your best version of you.

Set Your Goals

TO ACHIEVING THE PRACTICAL POINTS

GOALS	STEPS
	☐
	☐
POTENTIAL PROBLEMS	☐
	☐
	☐
STRATEGIES	☐
	☐
	☐
	☐
	☐

PROGRESS TRACKER

Date	Progress

DAY 46

"I Make a Difference in the World by Existing and Walking in my Purpose."

"Commit your work to the Lord, and your plans will be established."

PROVERBS 16:3

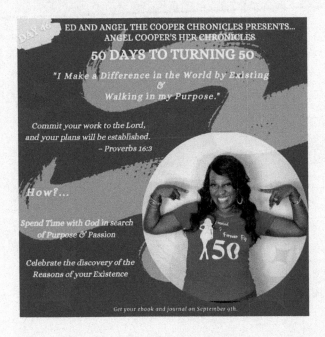

ED AND ANGEL THE COOPER CHRONICLES PRESENTS...
ANGEL COOPER'S HER CHRONICLES

50 DAYS TO TURNING 50

"I Make a Difference in the World by Existing
&
Walking in my Purpose."

Commit your work to the Lord,
and your plans will be established.
– Proverbs 16:3

How?...

Spend Time with God in search
of Purpose & Passion

Celebrate the discovery of the
Reasons of your Existence

Get your ebook and journal on September 9th.

FOUR PRACTICAL POINTS

- SPEND TIME WITH GOD IN SEARCH OF PURPOSE & PASSION
- CELEBRATE THE DISCOVERY OF THE REASONS OF YOUR EXISTENCE
- RECOGNIZE THE IMPORTANCE OF YOUR POSITIVE CONNECTIONS IN LIFE
- REMAIN CONSISTENT REST BUT DON'T QUIT

My initial reason for writing this book was to encourage people worldwide to share how to learn to reaffirm how God sees us. Understanding this principle can help inspire others to do the same. Bravely move in grace for this journey in life, even when it is complicated. While turning 50, I boldly began to allow God to heal me in my wounded areas. Which led me to walk tall in my purpose. It was not enough to look around to see what everyone else was doing then hope and wish. I had to move forward in my assignment after finding out my purpose. Moving forward, although I was afraid, frustrated, I did not give up.

Are you making a difference? Has someone's life been affected by you reaching back to pull them through their rough season? It is about impacting positive change for the future generation.

It is not enough to exist in this world. It is crucial to living the fullest in life and to live in expectation of God's blessings. Your children and legacy depend on you reaching your fullest potential and learning what it means to find your purpose in order to walk boldly and bravely in it. Regardless of your past or present circumstances, defy the odds with your God. Today's affirmation will provide strategies and practical approaches to be successful in this area.

Today's prayer is that the Lord speaks to your heart through the holy spirit so that I can hear from you, Lord, and know what to do. I desire to please you; I want to find my reason for existence to make effective change in this world. Thank you for guiding me. Thank you for loving me. Thank you for allowing me to walk in the divine purpose and plan for my life. In Jesus' name, Amen.

Set Your Goals

TO ACHIEVING THE PRACTICAL POINTS

GOALS	STEPS
	☐
	☐
POTENTIAL PROBLEMS	☐
	☐
	☐
STRATEGIES	☐
	☐
	☐
	☐

PROGRESS TRACKER

Date	Progress

DAY 47

"My Past is Not a Reflection of My Future."

"For I know the thoughts that I think toward you, saith the Lord, thoughts of peace, and not of evil, to give you an expected end."

JEREMIAH 29:11

FOUR PRACTICAL POINTS

- EVERY EXPERIENCE SHAPES YOUR FUTURE
- DEDICATED TO PERSONAL GROWTH AND CHANGE
- REMAIN CONSISTENT IN ACTION
- EMBRACE EVERY LEVEL OF GREATNESS ON YOUR JOURNEY

"The wound is not my fault, but the healing is my responsibility". This is a quote I read online that made so much sense. Most people only remember you from your past mistakes or trauma. They do not recognize the new person you have transformed into.

There are things out of your control that has happened to you. If someone abused you, assaulted you, or took advantage of you, it's not a reflection of you. I need to encourage you that it's okay. It was not your fault or responsibility. It was their evilness inside them, they will have to answer, and pay for wrongs inflicted on you in this life of the next.

Today, I want you to understand that there are some things that may be in your past that will not determine your future. It is the actions you take now or non-actions that willdetermine where you are going. We all have made bad choices and mistakes, but it does not mean you are a mistake. As our friend Job in the Bible, he did nothing to warrant his struggle. He did ask God for strength in order to see a more significant purpose waiting for him if he endured.

Do not allow your past to have a grip on your current life, placing constraints on you, mentally, spiritually, and physically. Most of the time, we do not understand that we can take power back through Jesus Christ and walk in the newness of life. I declare and decree that the shackles be broken off and every chained part of your life in Jesus' name. Your mind, heart, and soul are free to live in the great expectations of what God has in store for you. There is something powerful when you forgive yourself for your past mistakes and forgive those who have caused you harm. Release and let go of anything that works against your peace with God. All things are possible, like healing and victory. Please understand your past is not a reflection of your future. Today's scripture declares "I know the plans I have for you, declares the Lord, plans to prosper you and not to harm you, plans to give you hope and a future (Jeremiah 29:11). Practice trusting God with all your plans, dreams, and life.

Set Your Goals

TO ACHIEVING THE PRACTICAL POINTS

GOALS	STEPS
	☐
	☐
POTENTIAL PROBLEMS	☐
	☐
	☐
	☐
STRATEGIES	☐
	☐
	☐
	☐

PROGRESS TRACKER	
Date	Progress

DAY 48

"My Body is Healthy, My Mind is Healthy and I'm in a Healthy Place."

"And our completeness is now found in him. We are filled with God as Christ's fullness overflows within us."

COLOSSIANS 2:10

FOUR PRACTICAL POINTS

- HAVING SELF & SOUL LOVE
- HAVING CLARITY IN THOUGHTS
- HAVING AN AWARENESS OF REACTIONS & RESPONSES
- HAVING SPIRITUAL HEALING TAKES PLACE

Often in life, we disrespect our bodies and minds expecting them to operate appropriately.
When they begin to fail us, we get upset then try to fix them by giving them both proper nutrition. Today, we have experienced the most deaths and disappointments from the pandemic, illnesses, and the fall of family structure. It is crucial to take the time, not only to declare our mind and body are healed. It requires us to become intentional about treating ourselves with the proper care. You only get one body to live in so treat your body wisely.

Maintaining a physical, mental and spiritual function is important. When one is offline, the rest of your body is affected. When you are feeling off-center, take the time to refocus or reset. As you are working towards this healthy place, I encourage you to declare my body is healthy, my mind is healthy and I am in a healthy place.

There was a story in the Bible regarding God declaring healing for a group of lepers. Christ spoke to them from afar, he healed them and provided instruction, saying, "now go show yourself to the priest". It was in the education that healing occurred, pursuing Christ's design for your life and going forth in achieving a healthy place, mind, body, and spirit. Please read Matthew 8; "as they went, they were healed". It shall be the same for you; continue to move forth to your complete healing.

TODAY'S AFFIRMATION & DECLARATION

Set Your Goals

TO ACHIEVING THE PRACTICAL POINTS

GOALS	STEPS

POTENTIAL PROBLEMS

STRATEGIES

- [ ]
- [ ]
- [ ]
- [ ]
- [ ]
- [ ]
- [ ]
- [ ]
- [ ]
- [ ]

PROGRESS TRACKER

Date	Progress

DAY 49

"My Life is A Gift and I Appreciate Everything I Have."

"For by grace are ye saved through faith; and that not of yourselves: it is the gift of God."

EPHESIANS 2:8

FOUR PRACTICAL POINTS

- ALLOW QUIET TIME WITH GOD
- ACKNOWLEDGE YOU NEED HIS GUIDANCE
- ADMIT YOU DON'T HAVE ALL THE ANSWERS & YOU WANT HIS HELP
- ATTITUDE OF GRATITUDE WILL OPEN AN OVERFLOW OF BLESSINGS

The greatest gifts will not come in a box with bows or tissue paper. It is the gift of life.

Life is precious and is truly a gift from God. I am a daddy's girl. I remember the night before my dad, Pastor and friend passed away. It was the Saturday night before Father's Day. We were watching a movie and sharing our plans to celebrate him the next day. The following day, I received a call from my mom that dad would not wake up. Each year is a reminder to celebrate every birthday because you never know if it will be your last time together.

It has now been about 15 years since my dad's passing, which does not seem that long ago. Life has a brand new meaning of appreciating all of life. My dad's abrupt death is how God called him back to himself and how he left this world. Learning to live life to the fullest with the gift God has given you, requires you to cherish the time you have or spent. When you start to appreciate the little things, it becomes much.

Remain mindful of the time shared with the ones you love; it is a gift. Remain thankful and celebrate all of your wins. As David did when he danced in the city to celebrate a victory or win. Read 2 Samuel 6. Celebrate the life and your achievements. Always request God's guidance and instruction for your life and show appreciation for everything he has done.

Set Your Goals

TO ACHIEVING THE PRACTICAL POINTS

GOALS	STEPS
	☐
	☐
	☐
POTENTIAL PROBLEMS	☐
	☐
	☐
	☐
STRATEGIES	☐
	☐
	☐

PROGRESS TRACKER

Date	Progress

DAY 50

"I am Favored, Focused, and Fierce."

"For the Lord God is a sun and shield; the Lord bestows favor and honor; no good thing does he withhold from those whose walk is blameless."

PSALM 84:11

FOUR PRACTICAL POINTS

- LOVE GOD WITH ALL YOUR HEART
- HATE WHAT BREAKS THE HEART OF GOD
- STEADFAST IN HUMILITY RELEASES THE PROVISION OF GOD
- REMAINING FAITHFUL TO GOD'S PLAN

"Favored, Focused, and Fierce" is a declaration of God's power at work for us at any age. In getting older, many people give up or cancel out in life. Life is not over when you get older. The 50 affirmations and declarations will transform your life into manifesting the full blessings and favors. It is not over, even if you're experiencing a layover of your blessings. It is in our waiting that we learn what to do while we wait. Learning to wait with patience in prayer, praise, and a reminder of the promises of God on repeat.

Having a relationship with God helps us move and see things differently. It is the relationship that connects us to the promises of God that are over our lives. As we recognized, it is both the good and the bad in life that creates our total being as an individual. Our response will determine our outcome.

I want you to never give up during your darkest time and remember his promises to us. I can never stress that enough! Remember his promises! Overcoming power and strength is yours by affirming and reaffirming God's promises over your life. You are wonderfully and fearfully made in God's image. Use these affirmations and declarations daily to remind yourself. You are favored, you will remain focused on your goals and you are fervent, strength makes you fierce.

Set Your Goals

TO ACHIEVING THE PRACTICAL POINTS

GOALS	STEPS
	☐
	☐
POTENTIAL PROBLEMS	☐
	☐
	☐
	☐
STRATEGIES	☐
	☐
	☐

PROGRESS TRACKER

Date	Progress

About the Author

Lydia Angel Cooper is the quintessential woman. She is a wife, mother, daughter, sister, aunt, cousin, singer, worship leader, ordained minister, motivational speaker, and entrepreneur.

She is admired wherever she goes. She is the loving wife of retired RI Deputy Sheriff Edward Cooper, caring mother of three wonderful children, Edward, Angela, and Anelle. Born and raised in Providence, Rhode Island, Lydia Angel Cooper began singing and loving God at the early age of 4 years old at her home church. By the time she was 14 years old, she had formed a group called the Youth Singers for Christ (YSFC) which included her cousins and sisters, Rosalind and Melody. Now with her sisters, Lydia sings with a music group called Refined313. Refined313 has provided background vocals for Grammy Award-winning artists such as Michael Buble, Earth Wind, and Fire along with many more. As well as provided opening performances for Byron Cage, Isaac Carree, Mary Mary, and others. Refined has also worked with Ambassador Dr. Bobby Jones together and traveled internationally to the Island of Barbados.

Lydia graduated from Central High School in Providence, RI, and later attended CCRI obtaining her Associate's Degree in Business Administration. She received her Bachelor's Degree from College Unbound Program in Leadership Organizational Studies. Lydia received a certificate of completion in theater as well as becoming a certified life and relationship coach.

Lydia retired from public service after working in the Providence School Department for 25 years. Currently, she is co-founder of Dalem Security Services providing personal and commercial security. She is also part owner of Ed and Angel The Cooper Chronicles offering inspiration and motivation for marriages and relationships through online coaching sessions. Lydia is the co-author of the well-known book "Love is Worth the Work" and soon to be released "Crisis and Chaos on Commodore". Elder Lydia Angel Cooper conducts worship seminars for many churches. The Cooper family's spiritual covering is under the leadership of Pastor and Dr. Miller of Shekinah Family Worship Center in Providence, RI.

Lydia Angel Cooper has the heart to worship and praise God which is a true testament and symbol of what God can do when you trust in him. Her favorite scripture is Proverbs 3:5-6, "Trust in the Lord with all thine heart and lean not unto thine own understanding, In all of your ways, acknowledge the Lord and He will direct your path." She is committed to the art of excellence and loving all people to bring them to the knowledge of God. Her inspiration and presentation are anointed and breathtaking. She seeks to create and bring forth a clear message, "That Jesus Saves!"

Get the "I am Favored, Focused, and Fierce" journal to support you as read through "I am Favored, Focused, and Fierce" a book of affirmations.

Don't forget to visit
EdandAngelthecooperchronicles.com

Did you get the "I am Favored, Focused, and Fierce" affirmation book and journal?

Don't forget! You can re-watch the live videos on YouTube with your books!

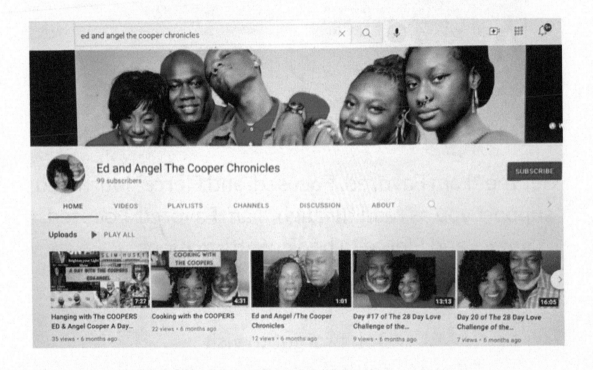

Visit
www.youtube.com/edandangelthecooperchronicles.com